Praise for CURTIS WHITE

"Curtis White's fiction presents a scintillant, ironic surface, one that is barely able to contain the bleakness of American *fin-de-siècle* exhaustion, which latter is his essential theme. It is a superb work."
—Gilbert Sorrentino

"Witheringly smart, grotesquely funny, grimly comprehensive, and so moving as to be wrenching."
—David Foster Wallace

"Curtis White writes out of an admirable intellectual sophistication combined with viscerality, pain, and humor."
—John Barth

"Like many other satirists . . . White is a moralist. . . . He also has the candor and—more important—the writerly grace never to let his characters' high-octane, obsessive monologues slide into leaden didacticism."
—Chris Lehmann, *Washington Post*

Other Books by CURTIS WHITE

America's Magic Mountain
Anarcho-Hindu
Heretical Songs
Memories of My Father Watching TV
Metaphysics in the Midwest
The Middle Mind: Why Americans Don't Think for Themselves
Monstrous Possibility: An Invitation to Literary Politics
Requiem

Curtis White

The Idea of Home

Dalkey Archive Press

NORMAL · LONDON

The Names of real people, living or historical, have been used in this novel.
None of these people did or said any of the things attributed to them herein.

First published by Sun & Moon Press, 1992
Copyright © 1992 by Curtis White
Cover art © Kamil Targosz <kamilt@hot.pl>

First Dalkey Archive edition, 2004

Acknowledgements:
"Tales of the Hippies" first appeared in *Witness;*
"Four Theses on the Fate of the Sixties" first appeared in *Clockwatch Review;*
"History Is the Debris of Duality" first appeared in *The Exquisite Corpse.*

Library of Congress Cataloging-in-Publication Data:

White Curtis, 1951-
    The idea of home / Curtis White.
        p. cm.
    ISBN: 1-56478-370-7 (alk. paper)
        1. San Lorenzo (Calif.)—Fiction. 2. Suburban life—Fiction. I. Title.

PS3573.H4575I3 2004
813'.54—dc22

                                                          2004053774

Partially funded by a grant from the Illinois Arts Council, a state agency.

Dalkey Archive Press is a nonprofit organization located in Milner Library at
Illinois State University and distributed in the UK by
Turnaround Publisher Services Ltd. (London).

www.centerforbookculture.org

Printed on permanent/durable acid-free paper and bound in
the United States of America.

CONTENTS

AN AVAILABLE WORLD

"It is even part of my good fortune not to be a house-owner."

—Nietzsche

This is Not an Autobiographical Statement

I would like, in this book, to imagine a place in which humans can live. A place more desirable than the failure which we presently inhabit. This failure which, we fear, cannot be defeated. I will admit that my purpose is utopian if that won't mean that my purpose is laughable. To be sure that it's not, then, let's be sober about our utopia. Let's understand by it the simple notion that there are ideas as yet unrealized which if realized would transcend our present reality.

This means that the town in which I grew up, San Lorenzo, California, is not a "place" where "humans" "live." A shocking proposition, no doubt, for those who have lived a lifetime on Via Segundo or Paseo Grande or Via Andeta or any other Spanish street for anglophones. And surely Gladys Best of 15751 Via Lunado would be appalled to learn that no one is "at home" in San Lorenzo. Gladys wrote in *The San Lorenzo Sun* in 1947 that "The inspiration of any artist would be a visit to our village of San Lorenzo." The only drawback she saw in "our little village" was the line at the post office.

Of course, she was right, there was something utopic about the founding of San Lorenzo. It provided what many people who had just finished fighting a war deserved yet didn't have: homes. In fact, the motto for *The San Lorenzo Sun* was "Where there is no vision, the people perish." I agree.

Speaking of vision, one of the great things about utopia is the terrific view. Do you remember Miss Nancy on Romper Room, how she was able to see us all on the other end of the television waves through her Magic Mirror? My sisters and I never doubted it for a moment; we surely felt seen, splayed before the TV's eye in our flannel pj's. Of course, our television screen, too, was a magic mirror where I was he as you were he and we were all together. Well, the view from this place I have in mind is even better than that! It's a place from which San Lorenzo can be seen quite clearly. Which can only mean that San Lorenzo isn't "in" the "place."

Sorry, Mrs. Best.

In fact, San Lorenzo is so far from the place that it is, as Maynard Krebs always sagely maintained, "nowheresville." Of course, Krebs and Thomas More referred to different "nowheres." Let me put it this way, I'm after a real nowhere. A realizable illusion.

An aerial view of San Lorenzo from a conceptual distance:

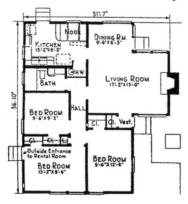

San Lorenzo's utopic purpose was not lost upon me when I was young. There was, after all, Little League. In fact, in 1960 San Lorenzo had the largest, best funded, best run Little League in the country. In the whole USA. Four grassy diamonds with fences all around, colorful handpainted advertising everywhere and a beatific snack bar where you could get rainbow sno-cones and bricks of candied popcorn. The San Lorenzo Dad's Club came out and painted the fences and hammered nails into everything. No one had it better.

I remember the day I got my first hit. I was eleven, a bench-warmer, and we were getting licked by Cuddy ("Cruddy") Plumbing. So I got to bat. Their pitcher put a not-so-fast fastball up in my eyes, I swung and ripped a ball into the left-center gap and through to the wall. I was nearly too stunned to run. But a poorish throw by the left fielder allowed me to stumble into second with a double.

I had other, different, shall we say, experiences as well. At tryouts one year, we were all told to stay away from the batter's box, back behind the fence. I made a casual calculation of the physics of injury and concluded that the chances of intersection for myself and the trajectory of a ball struck with any force were mighty small. Tiny. So I strayed onto the dismal side of the fence. But as with statistical theories of history, there was a flaw in my thinking. For just as the presence of ninety-nine white balls does not explain why blind-folded Lady Luck picks the one black ball, so my calculations could do little to deny the force of a ball tortured lopsided by the brutality of some thug's swing impinging with the fortunately thick boney plate between my eyes.

But, as I said, that incident had only to do with physics, dumb Newtonian mechanics. Nothing more could be inferred from it than a stupefying fatalism, and I continue to resist the idea that a malevolent material universe has it in for us.

11

Another time, I was photographed by a reporter for *The Hayward Daily Review* as I played third base. Sunday morning all my newspaper buddies piled their extra copies on my front step. It was pretty exciting stuff for a twelve-year-old. But at the next team practice, son of a gun, my coach had a copy of the photo too. He used it to show the rest of the team how completely out of position I was. He used it to illustrate our generally sloppy attitude toward the game, which was finally settled upon as a sufficient reason for why we were 3-7. I was told that I wouldn't be starting the next game.

That incident seemed even then to carry a force of irony that implied truths well beyond me, San Lorenzo and Little League. It was, I can say now, morally metaphysical.

And then, finally, there was the time my dad tried to help me with my swing. I was "hitching." So he said, "Maybe if it costs you a quarter every time you hitch, you'll be more careful about it." I admit, twenty-five cents meant a lot to me, but I didn't yet know how to allow money to improve me or my hitting technique. So, during my first at bat in a game with U. S. Market, I hitched, swung and missed.

"That will cost you a quarter," Dad yelled out from the suddenly green stands behind home plate.

I was angry. The other parents (especially the mothers) were horrified. I swung furiously at the next two pitches and struck out.

But I gained something in going down on strikes, whiffing before the world, failing so deliberately. My indignant humiliation prepared me for a future recognition of what Marx called "political economy."

I don't remember if Dad ever actually kept back that quarter or not.

□

You will be surprised to learn that there have been others who have lived in San Lorenzo and spoken of utopia. Around the turn of the century there lived here one Agapius Honcharenko of Ukraina, a priest in the Greek Orthodox Church, who had come to California to escape the political persecution of some combination of European autocrats. He was a remarkable man. He had heard the confessions of Count Leo Tolstoy. He had prepared a Russian translation of the U.S. constitution and then had it smuggled into Russia. And he had founded the bilingual *Alaska Herald* which attacked the "unblushing rascality perpetrated by monopolists" for whom he prescribed the "application of the Russian Knout." Whatever that was.

For his efforts, he received equally colorful replies. As one polemicist wrote, "This weed-snake, this sugar-clad human pill, this incarnate bad smell, tip toeing silently up to honest noses is the most nearly complete in all his appointments of any merely mortal nuisance with which this unhappy state is afflicted." Boy, if all reactionaries were that inventive, you'd join them just for the fun. Weed-snake indeed!

Anyhow, Honcharenko eventually settled in the barren hills east of Hayward where in hillside caves he raised exotic mushrooms and conducted religious services. Free from the duty of dragging the "dark doings" of capitalists into the "light of day," he had time for long strolls in the area. When he took a trolley into San Lorenzo, he got off at the Four Corners and walked down Lewelling Blvd., past the resort and picnic grounds, past the wealthy estates, towards Roberts Landing. Therefore, he walked right past the future site, the selfsame parcel of ground, on which stands the San Lorenzo

13

Little League. Being a visionary and a connoisseur of mushrooms, he might have been arrested in his walk by an anachronistic sound. A call from the future. A sort of clacking. The sound of bat on ball. Unworldly though such an experience would have been for him, my own more appropriate experiences in that place, I am trying to say, were no less bewildering. For when I return there and stand near the now tiny-seeming diamonds, at a distance no less phantasmal than Honcharenko's, I too hear the "crack of the bat." I see the boys in their uniforms with their little mutilated mitts dangling from their wrists. I see the fathers striding behind with their hands in their gabardines. And I feel a kind of disappointment, indistinguishable from personal failure, that Agapius Honcharenko—he who sought "revenge on the wolves that devour the lambs"— would have understood very well.

As Karl Marx wrote, the philosopher "merely makes objective the relation between his particular consciousness and the real world." That is to say, one begins at home, begins with a description of personal misery. Of course, it is not difficult to discover personal misery. I figured it out in the fourth grade. At San Lorenzo Elementary School, when you got to the fourth grade you could run for student office. The fourth graders nominated kids for treasurer. Of course, it didn't make any damned sense because nobody had any money to treasure. All we knew about money was that quarters from our parents ebbed and flowed depending upon whether we were "good" or "bad." And, of course, no sixth grader in her right mind was going to hand over allowance money for a fourth grader to take care of. Obviously, "treasurer" was an office through which we learned about offices and how to run for them.

And thus it was that, lo, in my ninth year, I too was one of those who "ran." I had a pretty good campaign. A great slogan: "Do what's right and vote for White." (Unfortunately, that still sounds like my immodest motto.) The only thing that I didn't understand was the student assembly at which I was expected to make a speech. Now, I'm sure I knew that it was coming and I think I knew what was expected of me, but no one there that day could have guessed that.

On the day of the assembly, the multipurpose room was lined with little oak chairs and smelled of sour milk and fish sticks. The boys had their blue jeans rolled up at the cuff. There was abuse in the air. I sat up on the stage with the other candidates and we were introduced by the outgoing student president, Katy something, a sixth grader who was most impressive and intimidating because she already had breasts. Finally, I was announced to the audience. I managed to walk to the microphone, but that's all I managed. I said nothing. President Katy, that monster of capability, whispered, "Say your name. Say your name." What a ridiculous suggestion: I didn't know my name! She must have thought I could get out of my fix by summoning myself like you call your dog, "Here, Bonzo! Good boy!" Now, if there was a me more me-like behind me to make an appearance, I certainly would have appreciated it. But it was strictly no-show. And, as far as I'm concerned, this quintessence of Curt has yet to put in an appearance. Maybe he's shy. Maybe he forgot we were having a party. Should we turn on the Late Show and stay up all night in case he arrives late?

As we are all obliged eventually to admit, the Self is an interesting abyss to fill. But fill it with what? The dread bestowed upon us by the Culture of Fathers? The "crappy shit" (as an amusing and wrathful Marx put it) of capitalist industry? Whatever we choose, in choosing we will have risked our lives on the idea (the very Notion which makes utopia) that it is possible to live a "better" life, to see and understand things "better" than others. Better, certainly, than our mothers and fathers, still residing in our first home, who can only be dead to us now.

Boy Finds Body

"Uncontrolled death can be a very serious interruption
to our progress towards liberation and enlightenment."
—Geshe Kelsang Gyatso, *The Heart of Wisdom*

I never found a body when I was a boy. So I can't write a strictly autobiographical story about a youthful "intimation of mortality" of that kind. But I've always felt like I should have at some time stumbled across a body. That is, my life seems to me informed by such an encounter. In the same way, I never saw my mother and father "doing the deed" either, and yet the Oedipal scene is no small part of my consciousness. Of course, we wouldn't have Freudian dreams or intimations at all if they weren't first provided for us in great detail. "First you need a Phallic Thing, like a totem pole maybe. Really, a pan of cocktail weenies will do. Then this haughty beauty comes over and munches the weenies down." It takes quite a bit of dream practice to get the trauma just right. The really stupid thing about it is that after all that work at constituting the "unconscious," all one is left with are anxieties, therapist bills and "insights" to pick at, like worrying a chicken wing for a sliver of flesh that simply isn't there.

At any rate, I've made a long study of this death business. It first occurred to me as an object of study when I was ten years old. I was playing soldier in the yard after dinner, in a nice quiet suburb, the calls of mothers lacing the air—"Vera!" "Chuck!" "Dave!" "Come in for dinner!" I had this terrific toy hand grenade and I was ducking down behind a redwood planter, loaded with stinky geraniums and loathsome garden snails, as if it were the lip of a fox hole. I was chucking the grenade at Kraut-Japs with that stiff-armed lob you used to see on *Combat*. This hand grenade was also a squirt "gun." If you filled it with water, pulled off the cap and squeezed hard, you got a potent stream. I, personally, never used it for that purpose. That seemed to me to cheapen the terrific realistic grenade presence.

Well, one of my grenade tosses went a little farther than I intended. It hit the top of our cyclone fence, like a triple to left center, but then bounced over to the other side—home run!—and rolled down the embankment toward the slimy green trickle of San Lorenzo Creek. It was a mistake and I regretted the toss because I really wasn't a very strong kid, and it was always a struggle for me to get over the fence, but since I couldn't take it back, what the heck, I enjoyed it for the moment—kaboom!—the grenade landed in the Nazi machine gun nest. The enemy bodies came popping up like toast.

Then came the depressing part: Me confronted with my inca-pacities. I could *not* climb fences. But I wanted my grenade back, so I dug my Keds hightops into the fence and grabbed the jangling and really painful metal and strained to the jagged top. Once on the other side, I saw that the grenade had hit on the slope and rolled into the creek itself and would probably have been three houses down the block by now if it hadn't caught behind the ear of a grey body. Yes, a corpse ear. The grenade stuttered there like a fishing bob. Actually, at first this "body" looked like an Electrolux vacuum cleaner that someone had thrown into the creek, but, no, that grey bag was really someone's shoulder.

Needless to say, I became suddenly much better at scaling fences (or cared less about the damages involved). I ran to the house to get my mom and dad, but where the hell were they? Not watching TV? The TV wasn't even on! Could this be my home? (Occasionally, in fact, a neighborhood kid would run in to the wrong house. After all, every house on the block was identical, so it was an easy mistake to make. Every floor plan was the same. The only difference was that alternate houses—rhyme scheme, A B A B—would have the floor plan reversed, as in a mirror image. So, you'd run in and— whoa!—it was the Alice effect, through the looking glass. What's wrong with this house? Why is the wall over there? You'd get queasy and seasick because the toilet was facing the wrong way.) But at that particular urgent moment, needing to tell my parents about a dead body, the alien appearance of the house doubled my feeling that there had been a horrible intrusion of the monstrous on the ordinary. I ran to the master bedroom, determined to find my own certain mommy, and burst through the door (perhaps this is why doors seem so sinister to me) just in time to see my pantless father remove himself from between the legs of my skirtless mother.

"Out, Buster!"

"I told you he wasn't going to play long."

"Out!"

Boy, I was really in trouble this time.

My father strode up the back walk barefooted, no shirt, just some khaki pants left over from his tour in the Japanese occupation. He opened the kitchen door and entered with a soggy, rusted, dented vacuum cleaner (a Hoover, not an Electrolux) held by the handle high in his right hand as if he were throttling a goose by the neck. Behind him, half messily out the screen door, was a black electric cord dragging like a string of the bird's shit.

"Uh-oh," my mother said.

"You idiot," my father said.

"Earl, don't call him an idiot. He is not an idiot."

"The boy doesn't use his head."

"But that doesn't make him an idiot. He just made a mistake."

"He thought a vacuum cleaner was a dead body. He don't make sense."

With my left hand I grabbed two fingers of my right hand and held them tight. I liked to hold my genitals in such anxious situations, but my mother had forbidden that. (Like when I would stand at the hallway door after my bedtime and try to watch just five minutes more of *Gunsmoke*, and my mom would say, "Stop playing with yourself and go to bed." And I would say, "I'm not playing with myself," and go to bed.)

So, there I stood bending under the sum of self-contempt which my father focused on me. (Even a Freudian could have told him it was an image of himself that stood before him, cringing in idiocy.) Bad as the moment was, there was a negative virtue in it. This scene could not have happened to just anybody at anytime. In fact, it could only have happened in the most narrow circumstances: Our own. How precisely the Depression and World War II and Vet Villages and a rotting laborsaving machine and a kid goofy from a contaminated form of play took their parts here. I'm not saying it wasn't pure pain at the time. I'd messed up. I was an Idiot. But now I can see that our time, our place, in short, our Spirit was involved in this. Hurtful and false though it might be in the moment, it

20

could also help move us along toward a very different result if we could learn how to let it.

And then there was the time that my Sunday school teacher (from one of the half-dozen ersatz, interdenominational neighborhood churches in our area) took a friend and me for a hike in the hills, out behind the Hayward Plunge. The Plunge was an enormous indoor swimming pool, shaped like an airplane hangar, built by the WPA in the 1930s. I hated swimming there, in part because I was a lousy swimmer, in part because it was dark, unnatural, and filled with violent confident city boys who jumped from unimaginably high diving boards. The place seemed dangerous. It seemed wrong.

But walking in the hills among the eucalyptus trees behind the Plunge was an innocent and easy thing to do. No problem: even I was confident about being able to hike. Just like walking, right? So, my friend David and I skipped ahead of this Sunday school drudge and had a good time. However, as we were going through a steep grove of eucalyptus I happened to see a body not fifteen feet down the hill. A black teenage boy in jeans, tee-shirt and sneakers with flies perching and strutting on his vacant eyes. David slid down to look closely and Mr. Sunday school came running in horror.

I turned to my teacher, feeling peculiarly experienced in these matters, and reassured him. "Don't worry. It's probably really just a vacuum cleaner or something," I said. "Right, Dave?"

My teacher then shared with me this look he reserved for the expression of moral disgust, and then one used to relay fear for spiritual health.

The next day the newspaper headlines read, "Boys Find Body."

21

One day, shortly after the vacuum cleaner disgrace, I was playing in the front—quietly, keeping all of my idiot assertions about the world to myself—when my father called to me from the backyard. What had I done this time? I walked around past the garbage can at the side gate and saw him leaning a ladder up against the house.

"Come on, Butch, over here."

Were we going to climb on the roof of our house? Why? I interpreted this odd desire as simply one more opportunity for humiliation: I wouldn't be able to climb the ladder. Or, if I made it to the top, I'd fall off. But my father was uncharacteristically helpful and encouraging and soon there we were, father and son, standing on top of the house for no very good reason.

Dad was in a peculiar mood. He seemed giddy, as if about to break out laughing. I looked down on our backyard, the corpse-less San Lorenzo Creek beyond it, the ballooning Burb next, and at the horizon of my vision the mud and tule flats of the bay out by Robert's Landing.

Then he put his arm around my scrawny shoulders and said, "Son, all of this will be yours some day." He laughed in a way I'd never heard him laugh before—full and committed to the belly of it—and he went on, "Well, maybe not everything, maybe not all those houses, not the creek there either, and maybe not the fence (city owns the fence). But that backyard, Son, and this house is all yours some day. Unless I take out a second mortgage, of course."

Then he laughed some more and I joined in, nervous at first but getting into the silliness, and when we almost lost our balance Mom came out to see what was going on and yelled up at us, "You two clowns! What are you doing on the roof, for Pete's sake? You'll break your necks, for cryin' out loud." She ran in to the kitchen and lured us down with tuna sandwiches and potted meat and Spam and chipped beef and sardines on saltines and our favorite corn chips with a pitcher of pink lemonade made the way we liked it with frozen lemon concentrate and we climbed down singing "Bob Ostrow the Maestro of delicatessen land! His luncheon meats are such a treat, they're always in demand!"

We sat on the lawn and ate our lunch picnic-style and when we kissed shreds of tuna and smudges of mayonnaise stuck to our cheeks.

"This is an interesting sandwich, dear," said Dad. "Isn't this cream cheese you've put on the tuna?"

"Yes!"

"And chopped green olives! Son, pay attention to what I'm about to say. LIFE IS BRAND SPANKING NEW. Well, isn't it?"

Life is new! Don't you wish your father had said that to you?

23

Willie Mays and the Idea of Home

"The stars, hum! hum!, the stars are only a gleaming leprosy in the sky."

—G.W.F. Hegel (quoted by Heinrich Heine)

Aldous Huxley once said, after allowing LSD to prop open one "door of perception," that he was able to see "the Absolute in the folds of a pair of flannel trousers." Which makes it not so strange to discover that one of the suburb's children, Chris (there were a lot of Chrises attending the grade schools, playing Little League and cutting classes in Walnut Creek and Fremont and Cupertino), understood Hegel's notion of *Sittlichkeit*—community—through the inspired play of Willie Mays. Willie Mays, cutting original figures in no-other-man's-land, the open spaces of center field. Of course, Chris didn't call it *Sittlichkeit*. He didn't call it anything.

Nonetheless, his intuition that Mays represented something special was uncanny and accurate. For Willie Mays was not just a star. He was a superstar.

"That's for sure," Chris said. "Do you remember the final game of the 1962 season? Talk about a hero! The San Francisco Giants were a game behind the Dodgers and needed a victory over the Houston Colt '45s combined with a Dodger loss to St. Louis in order to tie for the National League pennant and force the whole thing into a play-off. But the Giants were facing a hard-throwing right-hander in Dick Farrell, who'd already told the press, 'I don't intend to lose.' And the Dodgers were starting the always tough veteran Johnny Podres against the Cardinals in their new Chavez Ravine stadium."

"Boy, you really remember that day!"

"How could I forget! Those were the most important days of my life! Everything I know about love for others began there! But my mom did help me look some of this stuff up on microfilm at the library."

"Well, that doesn't matter so much. Your point is that this situation was pure drama."

"They were both terrific teams. The Dodgers could run (with Maury Wills, and Junior Gilliam and Willie Davis; even their catcher, Johnny Roseboro, had stolen home twice that year), but they were real weenies at the plate. I mean, those guys could not hit. On the other hand, the Giants had great sluggers. Mays, Cepeda, McCovey, Alou. They were bruisers like Sonny Liston. He'd hit some Bum of the Month in the shoulder and his whole arm would go numb."

"So, how did the games go?"

"Pitching duels. Farrell was as tough as he promised. He made a serious mistake with a fastball to Ed Bailey and Ed put one in the right-field seats. But that was it. However, Billy "Digger" O'Dell was no worse. He allowed only one scratch run himself. Going into the eighth it was 1-1. Then Mays came up with nobody on. He turned a Farrell fastball around and sent it over Candlestick's left-field fence. Giants win! Meanwhile, a 0-0 contest down in

L.A. was won by the Cardinals in the eighth on Gene Oliver's homer. Dodgers lose!"

"On to the play-offs."

"Yankees waiting for an opponent."

"They split the first two."

"The deciding third game is at Dodger Stadium. Going into the top of the ninth, the Dodgers sport a two run, 4-2 lead. Looks like they've got it. The Giants are grim. Sandy Koufax is folding World Series cashola into his wallet already."

"But, hey, the Giants still have three outs coming."

"That's right."

"Little Matty Alou pinch hits for Don Larsen and promptly stings an Ed Roebuck pitch into right field. Tying run is at the plate now, brother, and nobody out."

"Brings up ol' Harv Kuenn who nearly hits into a double play. Now he's on first. McCovey bats for Chuck Hiller and walks. Next, Felipe Alou walks to load the bases."

"Sounds like Roebuck was starting to stink pretty bad."

"And then up comes Mays and there's nothing to do but pitch to him. Walter Alston comes out to talk to Roebuck, but what can he say? 'Don't let him hit a homer'? I know what I would have said if I was Roebuck. 'Get me out of here! I don't wanna throw this pitch! Please, Mr. Custer!'"

"Very funny, Chris. So go on. I'm on the edge of your seat."

"Roebuck goes into the windup and here's the pitch (this is my Russ Hodges voice, not that Dodger-lover Vin Scully), Mays swings and crucifies the ball, it's a line drive, it's a rope, you could hang laundry on it, it's a home run condensed to the distance between himself and the pitcher's mound, it's a stick of dynamite in a shoe box...."

"In other words, Robert Oppenheimer would have been interested in this energy."

"Who's he?"

"Never mind."

"But Roebuck reaches out desperately and this terrific liner rips off his pitching hand."

"What?"

"It's lying on the mound now and the fans are getting sick. The Dodgers have really choked this time."

"I think you're stretching things."

"The Dodgers are falling apart."

"Chris!"

"Yeah Willie! Yeah Willie!" He's marching around, now, cheering to himself.

Well, the Giants went on to score three more runs to win the game and the pennant, humiliating the Dodgers 6-4. But that fact is not really what we're after here. Far more important is Chris' own situation that day. When he got out of school, he ran home and arrived in the seventh inning. His mom was already watching the game on their Philco hi-fi/TV.

"Hi, Mom. What's the score?"

"Oh, honey, it doesn't look too good. One of those stupid Dodgers just hit a home run. I think the score is 4-2."

"Think? Who hit it?"

"I don't know their names."

"Oh suck! Who's up?"

"Chris, don't say that word."

"What word?"

"Suck."

"Why not?"

"It sounds dirty."

"Suck?"

"Yes, suck."

"Why in the heck is suck dirty?"

"Just don't say it."

"Ed Roebuck! We can hit him. C'mon Giants!"

By the ninth inning, Chris and his mom were depressed. But Matty Alou's single cheered them. And when Mays singled in a run, and the Dodgers walked in a run, and wild pitched another one home, a beautiful thing happened. Chris and his mom leaped from their dusty chesterfield, grabbed each other by the hands and danced around the coffee table for the rest of the inning, screaming and hugging. Chris would always remember that moment.

"Always remember it! You're not getting this right. That was the moment when I learned what it means to be happy as a group. That's the only moment I ever felt at home. I mean, Home! It wasn't like I was happy because my report card said I 'Get Along Well with Others,' or a girl let me put my finger in her, or I wrote a book. I learned how to love other people then. I loved Willie Mays, I loved my mom, I loved what made us a team. Even now, it's only when I go to a ball game that I can talk to anybody at all and share something and be together and understand."

"I see."

"God, you really don't understand. No one understands me."

"I'm trying to understand."

"You're just one of them."

The condition of World Spirit, October 1962:

San Francisco	AB	R	H	RBI	Los Angeles	AB	R	H	RBI
Kueen, lf	5	1	2	1	Wills, ss	5	1	4	0
Hiller, 2b	3	0	1	0	Gilliam,2b	5	0	0	0
F. Alou, rf	4	1	1	0	Snider, lf	3	2	2	0
Mays, cf	3	1	1	1	T.Davis,3b	3	1	2	2
Cepeda,1b	4	0	1	1	Moon, 1b	3	0	0	0
Bailey, c	4	0	2	0	Howard,rf	4	0	0	1
Dvnprt,3b	4	0	1	1	Rosebro, c	3	0	0	0
Pagan, ss	5	1	2	0	W.Davis,cf	3	0	0	0
Marichal,p	2	1	1	0	Podres, p	2	0	0	0
Larsen, p	0	0	0	0	Roebuck,p	2	0	0	0
M.Alou,ph	1	0	1	0	Wlliams,p	0	0	0	0
Pierce, p	0	0	0	0	Prnoski, p	0	0	0	0

San Francisco 0 0 2 0 0 0 0 0 4 — 6
Los Angeles   0 0 0 1 0 2 1 0 0 — 4

San Francisco	IP	H	R	ER	Los Angeles	IP	H	R	ER
Marichal	7	8	4	3	Podres	5	9	2	1
Larsen (w)	1	0	0	0	Rbck (L)	3	4	4	3
Pierce	1	0	0	0	Williams	2/3	0	0	0
					Prnski	1/3	0	0	0

Chris spent the years following the Giants' triumph very strangely. While other boys were actually out playing baseball, growing strong, staying healthy, Chris retreated to his room ("the hermit's cave" his mom called it) where he replayed the 1962 season through a statistical baseball game he'd purchased with money earned by delivering the *San Leandro Morning News*. But it was the last of that money, because Chris quit the paper when he realized he could get in an extra five games before school if he wasn't out delivering papers.

His mom didn't object too much to his reclusive fantasies because she was sure it meant he had an interest in statistics. "You're going to be a statistician," she said. Although she had no idea what statisticians did, precisely, it sounded like a lot of money.

But Chris' perspective was far more exotic. Ecstasy had descended on him arbitrarily, unexpectedly. Through the Giants he had experienced triumph indistinguishable from love and innocent of ego. He wanted to live in that moment. He was an adolescent Trotskyite yearning for "permanent revolution." He wanted to get high and stay high. He wanted enlightenment. And so for most of his eleventh and twelfth years, he struggled to arrange for the game, the rolling dice—rattling like Tibetan skull-beads, thrown with all the solemnity of the I-Ching—to readmit him to utopia, to allow him not only his obsession, but control over it as well.

In spite of the fact that Chris stopped playing the game altogether when he and his hormones entered their teens, it is still too early to say whether he succeeded or failed in this quest. Because on the very day, the self-certain summer afternoon on which he emerged from his room knowing he would never play again, he walked into the living room, opened the filthy Venetian blinds and stared out the window. Under his gaze, the sidewalk endured as if someone intended to walk on it. Trees thrust out branches as if they were playing slide trombones. At last, his mother came up behind him and asked, "What on earth are you thinking about?"

"Skin," Chris replied with intensity. "Have you ever really thought about skin, Mom?"

"God, it's true," said Chris, laughing, "I was a pretty weird kid."

"It was an unsettling moment for your mom, too. Suddenly a mutant version of your future opened up for her. She couldn't tell if it was bad or good, but it scared her."

"Sorry, Mom."

"But enough about you and your mom. This story has another destination: your grandmother."

"My grandmother! Why are you going to write about my grandmother?"

"She's the one who moved the family to California and San Lorenzo in the first place. A gutsy move."

"Wait a minute. I thought we were talking about Willie Mays."

"True. But also about home. And it was Grandmother who made this bright burb home."

"Okay, but keep it straight or my family will disown me."

"It's probably already too late for that."

In 1945 Ella B., your grandmother, moved with her three already adult children from the trauma, poverty and heat of Depression era Kansas to the limpid possibilities of California, the San Francisco area, then booming with war production. And when the War Housing Center lifted its control over the orderly and glimmering community of San Lorenzo, she was among the first to buy one of the little homes. $5,950. Next to nothing down. Sycamore trees growing up and down the block. Juniper bushes, lilies, lawns, parks, new schools. Marvellous!

But, to tell you true, Ella felt a familiar despair in spite of all this good fortune, for it was rather late in life for one of her sensibility to be starting over, to hit fifty and have nothing more to show for it than another beginning. A new opportunity for failure. But a despair of this kind has a virtue, for it is spirit's prod. "You see how it is with time," it implies. "Time is insidious. Subtle. Understand something soon or die miserable."

Fortunately, Ella was not the sort to resort to pleasure and drink (she didn't hang out at Guido's—"Your favorite, mixed as you like it by Guido, Carl or Vic"); nor did she lapse into stoic calm (that *is* despair; that is pain you don't allow yourself to feel); she didn't even resort to the elaborate, gaudy subterfuge of art (jotting down poems or writing stories, "expressing" herself, each expression a betrayal, insufficient to its purpose). Instead, she shrewdly waited for something to happen that would stimulate recognition. In Willie's lingo, she "worked the count." It was three balls, no strikes. Sooner or later life was going to have to come to her with a fastball.

Of course, when this wisdom event happened it happened in a completely unimaginable way. As it ought. 1949 it was. A new department store had opened in the Village. A place called Mervyns.

Mervyns opened as the centerpiece of the new Village Shopping Center in 1949. It was owned and managed by young Mervin Morris, son to an already successful and wealthy family of California business-folk. Mervin, like many another sensitive rich-boy, was basically at a loss for something to do. Simply making money wasn't enough (although he'd make plenty in his time: by 1976, there would be thirty-five stores in the western states; by 1986, one hundred-seventy-five stores, as far east as Michigan). So when his father first suggested opening a department store, Mervin was not excited. But when he considered that it was to be in a new community, a place that called itself a "village" even after WWII's end-of-all-innocence, the idea became more attractive. And when he imagined the kind of central role he could have in this new beginning for vets, farm girls and their legions of children, it just all seemed good. They'd come to him by choice. He himself would spend some time each week selling on the floor. Children could get their shoes from him for two bucks. Brassieres for a buck. Knit girdles. Jeans. Socks. Special Purchases. 100% foam rubber things. He would be useful!

But Chris wasn't pleased. "I don't get it," he said. "This is really boring. I liked the stuff about the Giants better. I hated going to Mervyns when I was a kid. All my mother ever bought me was shoes and blue jeans, shoes and blue jeans."

Just keep your britches on, pardner. I'm getting to it. So, one day your grandmother was shopping at Mervyns, her first time in the store in fact. She was looking at this and that when this very pleasant young man came up and asked if he could help. She recognized him right away.

"Why, you're Mr. Morris, aren't you?"

"Yes, I am."

"Well, I'm so flattered."

They went on to talk about his plans for the community and Ella told him she was a teacher and volunteer with the Citizen's Aid Society. In short, they hit it off. By the end of their first chat, Mervin had volunteered to bring surplus goods from the store to Ella's house to be delivered to the Aid Society. There was also some suggestion of a meal.

Now, there was nothing romantic about this and never would be. Ella was twenty years older than Mervin. But I think each intuited that the other was someone he/she could have fun with without getting into trouble. So every Thursday afternoon Mervin would drive over with his convertible top down and some new toy from the store rising out of the back. Sometimes it was bikes and they would go riding up Hesperian into what remained of the peach orchards. Once it was a newfangled Coke machine and they set it up on the sidewalk and bought a Coke for every kid who came by. He also brought over redwood patio furniture, two thousand Easter bunnies, a sixteen-inch lawn mower with Sheffield steel cutting blades, tender rump roasts and skinless franks, percale and taffeta from the yardage section, and any other thing that made life more interesting than it was in fact.

"Didn't everybody think he was pretty weird driving around with all this stuff in his car?"

Yes. And at another time in another situation he might have suffered for his originality. But everybody was new to this San Lorenzo place and what was to be considered eccentric and what not was still fuzzy to most of the folk. Besides, the guy had a flair for bargains and white sales and such species of wonder. That alone would have kept people on his side.

So this went on for a good number of years. Then, one day in the spring of 1954, Mervin drove over and his back seat was full of televisions. Lord, you can bet all the neighborhood kids and their parents too came popping around like Mervin was Joe DiMaggio or dollar bills were flying out of his DeSoto. Well, seems like everybody helped carry the TVs into Ella's living room and extension cords were strung up and soon a sort of magic circle was created in which everyone on the whole block fit. It was exciting!

Then master of ceremonies Mervin Morris rose, his affection radiating from his little round face. He got the group's attention and said:

"Okay, everybody, turn the channel to 5…. Okay, everybody ready? When I say three, turn it on. On your mark…get set…one…two…three."

CLICKS.

I don't know what they were hoping for. Uncle Milty would surely have been welcome. Roy Rodgers, great. *Lucky Strike Cavalcade of Hits*, fantastic. And certainly they could have picked a better time of day. It was only noon, three o'clock Eastern time. Anything but prime.

At any rate, their euphoric hoorahs were followed by the grey, whispering image of a senate room and senators. It was the Army-McCarthy hearings, one of the first examples of live, in-depth (and sensational) public service broadcasting. The nation was transfixed by this exhibition of the Red threat whose other face was a familial evil. The face of Joe McCarthy dominated the screen, his voice whining and bathetic. Occasionally he let forth a high nervous giggle and gave a sidelong wheedling look into the camera and thus into Ella B.'s living room in San Lorenzo. He spoke.

"Point of order, Mr. Chairman. Point of order."

"Yes, Senator McCarthy."

"Has it occurred to the committee that we haven't yet ascertained information basic to knowing who our witness is? Let me ask you, Mr. Coleman, before your own Communist sympathies came out, did you consider the religious beliefs of your parents to be strong? Do you and your wife now attend services regularly? What party did you vote in the last election? What is your philosophy of life? Have you ever thought about whether public utilities should be owned by the government? Do you think the government should control labor unions? What are the four freedoms? Have you ever assisted in the invention of a freedom? Did your brother vote in the last election? Do you know how he voted? Wasn't your aunt sympathetic to bolsheviks? Do you support civil rights? Isn't education the basis of communism? Nothing to say, Mr. Coleman? Please, the loyal American public waits!"

This went on indefinitely. You can still catch it if you know the right time and channel. (It flickers on and off, an enduring loose connection in the national psyche.) Quickly, the little audience lost its enthusiasm. Everywhere they looked, all around them, the nasty talking head in the little box asked them questions. Finally, they began exchanging ashen looks and slipped in twos quietly from the room. They went back to their own little houses and shut the doors firmly. At last, Ella and Mervin were the only ones left. Ella's lips were trembling and she was about to cry when Mervin jumped up—it is not possible to fully appreciate the heroism and reckless-ness of this gesture—and began pulling out the electrical plugs from all the wall sockets.

Then he took Ella's hands and led her outside. "One more surprise, Ella! One more surprise!" He went to the car trunk and popped it open. Inside were baseball mitts and softballs. Hundreds of each mixed with each other like popcorn and cranberries.

"Dig in, Ella. Find one that fits."

She took the Ernie Banks model and ran over to the lawn. He grabbed the Whitey Ford then stared in for the sign.

Mervin wound up. "Here comes my spitter! Look out! My forkball! My roundhouse curve! Heads up! Bombs away! Geronimo!"

He threw it, a bit wide, and Ella leaped to her right and stabbed it, backhand, in the webbing.

"Nice catch, Grandma!"

You see, I knew you'd like this story.

36

UNNATURAL CHILDREN

"We find ourselves threatened by hordes of Yankee immigrants who have already begun to flock into our country and whose progress we cannot arrest. Already have the wagons of that perfidious people scaled the almost inaccessible summits of the Sierra Nevada, crossed the entire continent, and penetrated the fruitful valley of the Sacramento. What that astonishing people will next undertake I cannot say."

—Mexican Governor Pico, 1844

History of the Great Mouth

"In fact, of course, the 'productive' worker cares as much about the crappy shit he has to make as does the capitalist himself who employs him, and who also couldn't give a damn for the junk."

—Karl Marx, *Grundrisse*

Beyond his official ruthless skepticism, Allen McAfrica desired to understand the world as the World. Unfortunately, what he was most familiar with could only feed his skepticism: Southern California. Was Disney's Fantasyland supposed to provide a difference that would allow Los Angeles to be "Real"? Or: the Midwest. In the central Illinois town of Streator, civic leaders presently seek permission to construct a prison that will obscure the fact that the residents of Streator are themselves already incarcerated by their own narrow possibilities for being. And so there are factories to conceal the fact that no one makes anything. And there are Indian reservations to conceal the fact that we are all Indians. These things McAfrica understood in the way that only a Son of the Western Suburbs could. For McAfrica was from San Lorenzo, California,

Levittown West, "every lot a garden spot," a place where men and women from Kansas and Oregon had united in repose, found employment in re-tooled war industry, and set about the raising of families.

But even though McAfrica was born high and dry on the green front lawn of the not-necessary, he never lost his desire for "the World"—not the real world or the true world or the authentic world, but simply, as he put it, an available world that is itself. There was once a time when the World declared itself effortlessly, because others helped to provide it. A swart arm swept the bottles, glasses, the little plastic umbrella from that Bimbo's mai-tai, even the cigarette filth on to the floor and with one murderous jerk of the loins there was a riot goin' on; or Shanghai Lil was found and lifted to the walnut bar; or the folks made this big circle, right?, and suddenly we're all Zulus—you dig this jive?—and you're Johnny Cock-a-roo, strutting, shaking your wattles till the girls all cry, tossing that wigged-out top notch so that by the firelight it looks like you've got the Milky Way rippling from the top of your head; or it's just the kindergartners in a big sticky circle, but what Miss Clapmeister doesn't realize is that when they put their left foot in and their left foot out, they're doing that actual HOKEY-POKEY.

But it seems now that in order to have the space for the world, one has to reinvent the very possibility of space. Why, the last time McAfrica wanted a real scene, he had to drive a thousand miles, park his '66 Corvair on the very edge of the Oklahoma panhandle and take off walking across the Texas prairie, hundreds of miles, thinking the whole way, putting a rare Tibetan sort of intensity and excitement into it, knowing his trip had to take him to a very certain place in spirit as well as in geography. For it is by such investments in the unknown, the alien, that the world is regained.

That certain place, in fact, erupts backwardly some thirty miles south of Amarillo. The Texas high prairie pursues itself dumbly, a flatness untouched by the squattest humpling of an imaginable hill. It is mirrorly pent in infinite grit, in stuttering sagebrush. It is about as interesting as the back of your head.

And then, it happens.

As sudden as the surprising fission of an atom, the earth fissures, is cleft magnificently if somewhat randomly and a "canyon" erupts in that contradictory way employed by things which are grandly deep. It is miles across; its miles across are absolutely different: it wrinkles, peaks, valleys, curls like a dog's leg, and lifts like flesh. It is beautifully clear that this canyon, Palo Duro, is the cat's eye in the marble. You can hold it in your sweaty palm, you can roll it, play pockets-in-the-dirt with your friends. When you throw it in the air and see it framed against the blue, you realize that the world is this amazing mote that shares its destiny with a lot of other motes, and you are clinging to it as fiercely—and as precariously—as a dung beetle clings to his fecal ball. It is no wonder that the Egyptians placed him—original globe trotter—above even the jackal.

McAfrica said nothing of this to the pretty girl in the park ranger's booth. When she gave him a brochure, he fell in love with her left hand. He wanted to say, come on with me, sister. Let's envelope this big hole. Let's incorporate. But he had more important things to do.

He walked to the canyon floor, to the beginning of the Puzzling Argument trail which leads to distant Sanctioned Cruelty peak, around which pinnacle every deep desert scent returns brightly and from which the rigid canyon walls can be seen to whip in a breeze as fine as hammered silver. But to get there he had first to trek through those parts where the desert is smeared with its peculiar flotsam: the prickly pear, the frisking lizard, the effervescent palo verde whose droughty flowers are just as lurid as the humid forsythia's. And with each step the crush of oil oozed beneath his boot.

But as McAfrica climbed, he kept his disciplined eye inward turned, clapped to a promiscuous logic. There was a rigor in Mr. McAfrica's project you can't even imagine. Who was McAfrica after all? Where from? How came he by this legendary rigor?

He grew up in a suburb with a dog. That's all we know.

By the time the crest of Sanctioned Cruelty was in McAfrica's reach, the sky was a blue, molten and malicious line beyond it. A bit of granite clawed at his kidney, sandstone crumbled away leaving his fingertips frayed. But at just the last moment, just before falling away to a state of sandy unconstitution, he rose, as buoyant as the first slimy thing, the first patch of mucus and mud, the first snotty lung to claim earth and there he sat, perched on Old Cruelty's peak, gored fundamentally.

He looked around, it was so fantastic, and he said, "This is the most nothing I've ever seen."

"Well, the way I heard it told," began McAfrica, settled in now on his precipice, "this land was once the home of lolling giants whose knuckles were roast turkeys. At least that's how the Kiowa explained it to themselves, sitting around the vast tribal fires, inspired by one or more of the illuminating buds they gathered from the desert floor. Anyhow, these giants were fat buggers. They were so big and fat that they couldn't walk properly, so mostly they just reclined, only exerting themselves to reach into Montana to pluck up dinosaurs. But what's important to the tale I have to tell is that a thousand years after the passing of these behemoths, buffaloes rose from the simmering brown dumplings that the giants used to shit.

"It was in thanks for the bison—that dusky, humped lumberer—that the Indians of the southwest worshipped the autoch-thonous churls, the indolent lobsters, those giants, who were once chock-a-block, elbow-to-elbow in the prairie, but were now no more. They were gone, but their spirit and their generosity remained in the dungy buffs who provided so much for the welfare of the Indians.

"Thus, the reason that buffalo chips burn so brightly; for the essence of long ago Titans escapes from matter and streams back to the spirit world.

"But imagine now a thousand thousand of these noble, woolen lumps so thick on the plains that nothing else like landscape had been able to assert itself in a millennia. Just over there it was," pointing, "just beyond that northern ridge called 'Primitive Abstraction Rim' by the natives. From that point as far as the eye could see the bison gripped down tenaciously, God's shag carpet, for the ground was theirs! Till come-a-ki-yi-yip, whooping up behind charged Comanches, riding fast but looking a little silly on the tiny Spanish ponies their race had long ago received in exchange for ten thousand deaths by yellow fever, small pox and old Big Belch, Mr. Blunderbuss. Like children on scooters, their feet dangled to the ground so that often when a pony faltered the rider himself could keep them going for a stride or two.

"Not the image of ferocity, I agree. But anything that was not earth or dung could startle the buffalo. The sky could startle the buffalo. A prairie dog's squeak could put them in a frenzy. On the Indian's first approach their tiny hooves danced, they shifted their weight, meaty chests cracking, run away!, little creatures attack us!, a vast stumbling began, which spread like an ocean wave, or rolled like nausea, the high plains a churning stomach now, urging doomed buffalo before its puking Need.

"Now, the herds of buffalo had always lapped at the edges of Palo

Duro canyon. As the animals at the herd's extremes aged, they were naturally sloughed like dead skin into the gorge, where bison greybeards were swallowed up, abysmally, however furiously their legs pumped. (I see them falling stiffly, though, as if they were nickels that a child had tossed into the darkness.) There on the severe rocks below they were chawed, joint and tendon blasted, flesh exposed and portable for rat and coyote and every other varmint with a hunger. Yet, this was still called the world-at-peace, because not so many buffalo died that there was any accumulation, and at any given spot the feisty ground squirrels would already have exploited the last knuckle of bone for its tangy marrow long before the next delivery of bulky manna.

"However, this all changed, and earth history changed, on the day of which I speak, the day the Indians call Gluttony or the Big Stinking. For the first revulsion alone sent five hundred bison smashing to their deaths. Then the spasm grew, fed by grief and fate; from my seat here on Old Cruelty it must have looked like a shitten waterfall. A paradoxical light glimmered off their horns as they fell and, at the bottom, off moist bone, ball and socket which ripped through their pelts.

"When the Indians arrived at the rim, they were amazed and scared. Had they created this prodigy? Was their medicine so powerful? But think of all the grieving and the thanking to be done! They'd be up for nights. They looked down again to see the umber corpses piled high, the spires of cottonwoods barely managing to reach above their mass. This scene the shamans would call, in their stories, the many-beasts-not-beasts, the Absolute."

□

43

"Later, the Indians descended the serious cliff walls, their raw flesh screaming in the liquid canyon air. When they reached the bottom, though, it was another matter. They waded deep into the death of the buffalo and found it an awkward, unfamiliar business. Does one put one's foot on that slick thigh bone? Or trust the apparent massiveness of that belly? There were times when they discovered that beneath the shaggy hides there was nothing more massive than a strange dark jelly. And of course they had to be wary of faults in the topmost crust of bison. A false step, a tremor, an unpleasant jostling and—whisk!—young Badger's Snout was gone.

"But the hard part was done, the monumental alchemy achieved. Lethargy, apathy: they don't say enough. The appalling indifference of the dead. The buffalo had their very skins taken from them, their horns appropriated, their hams taken for drying into pemmican. But deep down in that bulk which spread across the canyon floor, which crested thirty feet up the canyon wall, resentment stewed against the agile red monkeys: they'd rue the day. Not now, maybe. But one day, when these thousands of buffalo corpses were nothing more than a peculiarly knotty sand, perhaps it would take that long, but someone would feel their clumsy wrath.

"It's with this in mind that I ask you now to consider a time, not all that distant, a mere hundred years, when in fact Indian fortunes had swung rather nastily."

McAfrica paused here to consider his precarious situation perched atop Sanctioned Cruelty. He'd like to pace and think for a moment about what he had to tell next: how the first Americans, like the buffalo, were in their turn absorbed by the thirsty southwest. But he knew he shouldn't move for fear of falling into the casserole of history which cooked slowly on the canyon floor. And he felt he couldn't move because Cruelty's spire had really sunk in him now. It hurt and it thrilled, and he couldn't deny it. Yes, a cushion would

44

have been nice. Then, he started it up again.

"Good god, can you imagine what the Nazis could have done with Palo Duro? Can you imagine what would have happened if Amarillo were the Warsaw ghetto? Whew! What they did with shovels and a few metaphors was deep enough. Or the Khmer Rouge? They stuffed an entire nation into an irrigation ditch. With a big bag like Palo Duro, they could have pulled the whole planet through, inside out, like reaching down and yanking a guy's intestines out through his nose. Oh, this is the killing floor, all right.

"But where were we? About to find out how the Indians got theirs, right? It's not a pretty story.

"Recall, by the 1870s, the Indian wars were near concluded. But in the panhandle area, the land of bad water, rugged cap rock escarpment, gypsum and buffalo wallows, several Indian tribes— the Kiowa, Cheyenne and Comanche—had gathered under Chief Quanah Parker for one last attempt to live outside of the reservations, with something like a native identity. Several things worked in their favor. There were no white settlements in the area and— because dust and heat were never more than a moment from absorbing anything with the arrogance to be moist and to live— there were not likely to be any settlements in the near future. And thus it would likely have remained were it not for the witless revenge of the buffalo.

"The queer thing about this drama—in which an entire continent boiled, slopped messily at the rim, spread its heat carelessly— is that its ultimate moment, the battle of Palo Duro, involved almost no loss of human life. Two, three Indians dead, one bugler wounded, that's all. A lot of 'sposed-to's-that-weren't created the situation. The Indians weren't supposed to leave the reservations, weren't supposed to hunt buffalo, were supposed to eat govern-

45

ment supplied beef. The white hunters weren't supposed to hunt buffalo south of the Arkansas River, by agreement with the Indian nation at Medicine Lodge.

"But the buffalo had been harvested from Kansas and Colorado by 1874, and, treaty or no treaty, the hunters considered that they would be more successful if they hunted buffalo where the buffalo were. So, into the panhandle they came with orders for thousands of hides from Mr. Lobenstine in New York. Amazing to consider: an 'order' is 'placed' and the history of a continent is changed. But, one admits, if it hadn't been the hide market, it would have been something else. For the idea of ranching, of long horns, chuck wagons, and little dogies getting along had already occurred to white men as a stern vision. Destiny. Moving the buffaloes and the Indians out would be difficult, but when it was done, there would be T-bone in Kansas City, rib eye in Frisco and St. Lou. It was hunger again, and the great mouth of the world, the Palo Duro gullet, was eager for its share of the chewing.

"I want to render this history precisely, so I'll start from the beginning. First, there was the canyon in its suchness, grandly deep, backwardly explosive, as I've said. Second, above the canyon a leisurely, crew cut expanse, the Texas prairie, covering thousands of square miles and with nothing more urgent on its hands than supporting a world of mid-grasses, such as the silver bluestem, the sand dropseed, the purple three-arm, and the colorful forbs like the Indian blanket, the globe-mallow, and the brazen humped ground-flaunt. Punctuating this radiant waste was the durable mesquite, a squat pretender to treeness, which grazing animals had brought up from Mexico (for the lucky-duck mesquite seed passes through the digestive tract of, say, a longhorn not only unharmed but with its seedcoat strategically scarified by gastric juices; thus upon its evacuation from a beast it is fertilized, watered and in all ways at

46

home). The mesquite's story provides an instance of genuine groundedness, of homeliness; it gives new vigor to the concept of 'native'.

"Now, folks, down there, tucked into the Palo Duro's colorful cleavage, were the teepees of the tribe of Quanah Parker. There were six hundred to a thousand warriors, as many more women and children, dogs, fifteen hundred horses…do you begin to see it, the Concept? OK: grass, canyon, Indians, and then look at the canyon rim and there ranged like spectators is a grand stand of the concerned but uninvolved. First, little guys in front, four hundred million prairie dogs from a grid of prairie dog towns twenty-five thousand square miles in range. Behind them the pronghorn antelope—thirty to forty million of 'em. Then the buff, another forty million. Believe me, it was standing room only in this so-called desert.

"It was only the whites who were insignificant in their numbers, in this place where almost nothing existed in less than millions. The reason for this is that there simply weren't many whites, although it is true that none of them dared to ranch or settle yet, not till this Indian misunderstanding was cleared up. So, there were only a few hundred buffalo hunters and a few hundred soldiers to protect them. Nevertheless, the fact is that among all the infinite, raw, bloody birthing of animals and Indians in the panhandle, millions upon millions of the newborn dropped upon the yielding bluestem grasses, not one single white child. But the whites did have a compensating if unfoundable quality which was absolutely the essential element of their race. It was nothing like the Right that the joining of blood and dirt bequeaths; rather, it was a promiscuous, productive delusion. It allowed them to create enormities, wonders.

"One of those wonders occurred on the 27th of September,

1874, when the command of Colonel Ranald Mackenzie came, at dawn, to the canyon of Palo Duro. There it was they stood, by that sandstone proboscis," again pointing. "Below they saw the Indian village where Quanah Parker and his braves slept with their herd of horses. Mackenzie's hope was, of course, for surprise, so down immediately he directed his command into the Palo Duro maw. However, a sentry standing just there, on that fleshy protuberance," another wild gesture, "saw the hated blue coats descending the turning path and so created an extraordinary warning while waving his red blanket vividly. Great Comanche warriors, K'yabeen and his brethren, scaled the canyon walls, took cover behind that breastwork of rock, and that one, and that one, sweet Jesus, they made it a pretty jaunt for Mackenzie's boys, and began to fire down on those soldiers and cavalrymen who had reached bottom. What the Indians hoped was to give others the time to gather equipment and, especially, to save the horses. But scouts and Beaumont's company A—ah, it's a stout lad that Aloysius Beaumont was—they penetrated the galling salvo coming down from the cliff-side and soon forced the braves to abandon the horses and flee through a pass in the western end of the canyon.

"And that was it. *Finis* battle. Needless to say, compared to the quantity of blood let in the Texas panhandle on just about any other day in the last fifteen thousand years, this 'battle' was as nothing. Nevertheless, it was defeat for the Indians, for without their horses they couldn't move camp, elude cavalry, or pursue buffalo. In short, they were unable to maintain themselves. So, back to the reservation they all—even the fierce Parker, the fiercer Isatai—went. Which leaves me with only the questionably historic tale of Private McGowan and his tobacco pouch to relate." This thought seemed to tickle McAfrica some and he wriggled on Old Cruelty's piercing rib like a catamite. "Now, it happened that one

48

Private McGowan had been unlucky enough to have his horse shot out from under him and he'd had to abandon it in order to save his own life. But after things had cooled some and the air was less splendid with lead, he walked back toward his mount—faithful, if dead, Authentic Freedom—in order to retrieve his tobacco and ammunition. As he bent over his erstwhile bronc, his not-steed (reduced in this bad hour to the .44 slug that had pierced her lungs and now paused, misshapen, against a sturdy rib) he noticed something, peripherally, in the low branches of a tree to his right. Then he saw her.

"'Well I be dogged,' he exclaimed, 'It's a dad blat lil girl.'

"In fact it was seven-year-old Snow Blossom, a Comanche child, niece to Quanah Parker himself, the very same girl who would be known in her later years as Thirty-three Kettles. But now nothing nearly so awesome, she was just a little girl whose lips trembled and eyes flooded like any other little girl's at a moment of horror and loss. She'd climbed the tree in panic and been left behind in the confusion, a fact which couldn't help but touch even a heart as box-like as Private McGowan's.

"'Great gawd, child, come on down. You cain't stay here by yourself. The wolves'll make you a lil tart after they eat up ole Authenticity there.' She clung to a limb, didn't budge.

"Realizing that he himself might be left behind in a few minutes, McGowan tried to climb after Little Kettle, but few of the limbs would hold his weight and she was agile enough to move quickly out of his reach when he struggled close. But McGowan was unwilling to leave her behind, however great the risk he placed himself in.

"'C'mon now, we've got to git. Colonel Mackenzie won't miss the likes of me and he won't wait, so we got to go. You don't have to be afraid, I ain't gonna hurtcha.'

49

"'But I am afraid,' she replied, as clear as the range that would in the next century be home to millions of anglophones. 'You whites eyes have a hunger bigger than the Big Stomach Canyon for all our buffalo but also for the children of the Comanches. My Uncle Quanah says so.'

"'You mean you think I'm gonna eat you?' our Private asked, for the moment missing the remarkable fact that she was speaking to him in English.

"'Yes.'

"'Well I be dogged,' he concluded.

"Now Private McGowan had a wife and little girl of his own up in Wichita, and what he decided was that this Indian child was likely to be charmed by the same things that charmed his daughter. So, taking off his belts and gun, he produced from a pouch a chaw of licorice which he passed up to a branch near Little Kettle. Then he put on his best show, the one that always left his own girl giggling through a licorice drool: a rousing version of 'Turkey in the Straw' sung while clogging madly, his belly bounding about, all punctuated by frequent heart-felt solos on a potato-whistle. Sure enough, in ten minutes time he had her chortling, her chin a-drip in black goo.

"Soon, she was down, raiding his bags for more licorice, and then they left, pig-a-back, returning to Colonel Mackenzie's stern column."

"But Colonel Mackenzie and his command were already gone. They couldn't dawdle in the canyon and risk being trapped, in their turn, between its indifferent walls. So, when Private McGowan and Little Kettle reached the ascending trail, there was no one. But not no thing. For Mackenzie's men had left behind what was astonishing to behold, the latest acknowledgment of Palo Duro's appetite, the still trembling accumulation of dead and dying horses that had been a herd of fourteen hundred only hours before. Their mass spread brownly, easy to clamber over if you would, but paralyzing to anyone who paused to consider.

"Little Kettle paused, began to whimper and McGowan feared he would lose her again to mistrust, suspicion of his relationship to such ways.

"'Now just hold on for one minute,' he insisted, 'there's an explanation for this somewheres, but if we're gonna hear it we got to go over this mess. So just let's get started.' He took her hand, swung her up on his shoulder and set his stalwart boot heel firmly on a nag's snout."

"Private McGowan and Little Kettle climbed those canyon walls together, and they followed the company's trail for the rest of that day and much of the next before they finally caught up to Mackenzie. They were healthy even though it had been a hard, hot walk. Most of the way they'd gone hand in hand, McGowan yarning about Pecos Bill and the like and Little Kettle expressing contempt for such lies, or McGowan lecturing her on staying near her mommy who was no doubt worried. But something disturbing happened. McGowan reported that he and Little Kettle—yes, I grant you, near delirious with heat and dehydration—saw something. Perhaps it was a mere phantasm, a mirage, a not-thing.

"But McGowan insisted—and you could hear him tell it as late as 1932 in the rest home near Satanta, Kansas, where the leeching soil had absorbed him at last—that he saw—and Thirty-three

Kettles would have corroborated if she were around and not the victim of her own dense years—the following:

"It was the sack-like form of a white woman who labored beside an umber lump, a tumorous bump, a dead buff. She was skinning it. With a pointed ripping knife she slit the hide from beneath the lower jaw, along the neck and down the belly to the tail. Then she ripped down the inside of each leg. Next, with a crescent shaped knife she cut around the neck, taking the ears but leaving the skin of the head for the bone beetles. Finally, with a rope noosed around the skin of the buffalo's neck and ears, she bore downward and with her enormous haunches bursting she grunted once and tore the hide from the fatty ligaments which held it to the carcass. The buff was left obese, naked, and obscenely pink, as if the earth had tossed him up unfinished, its nastiest secret.

"Then, as the sack-like figure rose, struggling beneath the heavy pelt, McGowan noticed that she was pregnant and near ready to deliver. Well, the remarkable fact is that in 1876 Mrs. Robert Truby, of Fort Griffin, would follow her husband to the buffalo range to perform the strenuous work of skinning. She skinned buff the day before her first child was born and returned to skinning the day after. You could have seen her involved in her work, straddling the buffalo pornographically while working at his soft belly with a piercing knife. Suddenly, a twinge. Mrs. Truby reaches under her leather apron and, with a shrug of wonder, removes a steaming infant. Wrapping him in a still bloody hide, she wipes her hands on her own wide thighs and begins ripping again. This child, Hank Smith Truby, was the first white child born in the Texas pan-handle. You almost certainly went to high school with one of his innumerable descendents. He was on the swim team. Or he played drums in a band that did 'Wipe Out' and covers of Jan and Dean tunes. His thick spit clung to the lip of a beer can you took a swig from."

And with that, McAfrica seemed to think he was done. The placid buzzing of his lips ceased. He sat upright as if suddenly aware that Old Cruelty's granite prod was no longer stimulating but, rather, hurt in a way not even he could describe. He got to his feet, flexed his stiffened legs and then, with no further reason for staying, started his descent down Puzzling Argument Trail.

Once back to his Corvair, he drove straight into Amarillo to spend the last buck-and-a-half to his name on beer. So he pulled into a little cantina he'd patronized in the past, the "Original Accumulation" (although it seemed to him that it had been called the "First Moment" when last he'd visited). He walked in and crossed over to the bar feeling a little like, yes, he might just be in the wrong place. In fact, he felt a bit like old Quanah himself, and like he'd wandered into something thick. Something he didn't quite understand. He remembered, then, that the First Moment had the head of an old buff mounted on the wall opposite the bar. He remembered that it was the head of a grizzled bull, more stupid than majestic. McAfrica turned and, yes, there it was. But something was different. Something was sunk into the buffalo's forehead. At first it looked like a silvery representation of a mushroom cloud, rising like this old buff's last and dumbest thought, no doubt placed there by some liberal-leaning wag. But as McAfrica peered, the object came to look more like a simple question mark, as if it had finally occurred to the bull that things were happening in his life that he didn't understand. Finally, McAfrica went over to look closely and saw that it was merely a small hatchet planted in his skull.

Returning to his seat, McAfrica found the bartender waiting with his beer. The bartender looked like an accountant or someone on the debate team who'd grown a little mustache as soon as he got away from the coach.

"Say," asked McAfrica, "wasn't this place once called the First Moment?"

"Boy, that goes way back, I guess," said mustache, smiling meaninglessly. "It's been the Original Accumulation since I've been here. Five years. It's true, though, every once in a while an old-timer will come in looking confused and ask if this isn't the First Moment. I never knew what the hell they meant."

So, McAfrica sat, exuding a complicated misery, feeling alienated in a place that should have felt like home. The people were strange here, too. It wasn't a racial strangeness, they were white enough; but it might have been that they were the cleanest white people he had ever seen. Here in the dustiest place in the world, they wore only white, or bright prints on white, as if they owned this place without having to touch it. McAfrica was not attracted, but he was curious.

Eventually, he managed to sit with them, even though they gave his chair and his aura of dirt plenty of its own space. Okay, then, it's true, he was attracted to them after all. They were—the boys and the girls alike—kind of sexy. Real sexy, in fact. They looked so edible. Ron was a regional sales director for Dun & Bradstreet down in Dallas. Martin was the hotshot coordinator of a software distribution concern in Phoenix. Sharon sold diversified stocks. Maureen was a corporate lawyer in Houston. But what most impressed McAfrica is that they were so beautiful to look at.

Marvelous to tell, as the evening progressed our adventurer discovered that Maureen was attracted to him, too.

"I know where you're coming from," she said to him at an advanced stage of the evening. "I've been there."

"Where?" asked our Mac, failing to notice that the Original Accumulation had become one of the darkest places in the Western Hemisphere.

"I mean, I know where your head's at," she continued, "and I admire you for it. I used to read the Castenada books, too. They were terrific, for the time, of course. I mean, being in touch with the primal directness of the land and all.

"But times change," Maureen explained, "And we've got new frontiers, new kinds of personal growth, new kinds of directness." Her face was vivid—almost sizzled—with this enthusiasm. "You see, there are no 'Bow-Tie-Daddies' here, right? That's what Zappa called them. Our parents' generation. And who's to say the energy we're in touch with is anything less than primal? I mean, the corporate world is an exciting place to be right now."

Later, at the evening's bleary climax, Maureen took McAfrica's hand under the table. He was astonished but unafraid. But when he looked over at her he understood that perhaps he should be afraid. For he hadn't noticed that Maureen wore a necklace on which an enormous bear claw dangled. And her eye shadow was a glimmer of fish scales. She had a crow feather in her hair.

"Mmmmm. You busy tonight, Keemosabe?" she asked. Then she brought his hand up under her skirt and locked it there, between her legs. He felt the shaggy mat of hair which spread down her thighs, the coarse patches of hardened filth. There was the stink of buff in the air.

McAfrica's panic was extreme, but his hand was locked tight.

She smiled and then in a fit of ennui yawned, right in his face, opening her mouth so wide you could hear the tendons and bones of her jaw stretch and crack.

Dig Here and You Will Find a Writing

Invocation: "Woe to he who will crush the senseless worm that crawls at evening in his pathway!"

The story I have to tell took place during the reign of the Legislature of a Thousand Drinks. I, Silkman, an aristocrat of cards, a high-toned sporting gentleman, saw it all transpire. I understand it now as clearly as your acey-deucey. I should have understood it then, since, in my incomparable Beau Brummel waistcoat, I had the ear and the confidence of every fat man on that august Legislature. But it is too late. It is a hundred years too late! I can only tell the tale now, and that only if I have time. For my bowels flee from me. They dissolve from the far side and flow from the near. My intestines mistake themselves for a fuse! That much, its sizzle, I can feel. The far margin of my intestine turns to dust and falls into the funnel. I am my own hourglass. The black grains pour from my fundament like gun powder from its keg.

I sit in a corn crib in the shadow of Mount Diablo. (I'm pure friction. I'm a live wire. Touch me and we all go, the devil's quaint volcano as well.) They have drained the swamp—on which I have

56

kept my gaze for these last fifty years—in order to develop houses. The whip-like rushes, the truncheon blooms of the tules are brown and dead. Twenty bulldozers, earthmovers, dump trucks gun their engines and will not stop. I think they are bug husks.

Invocation: Oblige to speech all plots to kill: the threatening demonstration of a dog's bark, arsenic in his medicine, laudanum in his coffee, chloroform on his pillow, several blows of a hammer on his head, heavy, dull blows with the axe, more dogs developing.

Silkman, your professor of cards, was handsome. Observe his patent leather, high-heeled boots, that costly diamond breast-pin. Observe the dainty diamonds on his fingers, sparkling withal. He was cordial, bland and fascinating. Even his toys were serious: he carried a derringer. Pint-sized death! On its ivory grip was inlaid lapis lazuli. On the one side, a bloody hand, hearts a-flushing. On the other, a twofold dilemma. His countenance gave advertisement of intellectual power, calm, reserved power. There was no mercy. He surely crushed the senseless worm that crawled at evening in his pathway.

I am Silkman! My body *is* this history. My body is deep with time. I keep to myself in these tules as a courtesy. I'm too profound to be looked at. For if you were to gaze at me, I might gaze back. Therefore, those bulldozers work at risky revelation. Sleepers awake! Give the bright eye of the sun but a moment to look on the ground cleared of the thoughtful tules and it will be obvious that the loblolly pattern in the hardened mud is the crisscross of bone on the top of my cranium. Dig there and you will find the book of my memory in which is a writing.

Thus:

In our beginning were the Acalanes, copper-colored people of peculiar habits. This district was infested by hordes of these creatures. The Legislature of a Thousand Drinks set their fine tables up on that breastwork of hills yonder and made their important judgment:

"The general expression of the wild Indian is indicative of timidity and stupidity. The men and children are absolutely and entirely naked, and the dress of the women is the least possible remove from nudity. In February and March they live on grass. Clover and wild pea-vine are among the best kind of their pasturage. We have often seen hundreds of them grazing together in a meadow like so many cattle. They are the descendants of Nebuchadnezzar. They live to die."

Invocation: Oh, you far removed race, you swarming infants, you who consort with death, you more willing to submit to kindness than negroes, your great disposition for extinction puzzles our dull brains. Your aptitude for cholera occupies the studious mind.

When the Acalanes vanished before the overwhelming tide of civilization, the world was rid of so much filth. But the dozers, working for these slim housing development boys, raise a tide that is itself filthy. The dusky vaqueros, that race half-caste of Castilian and Indian blood, might have been a clue if I'd had any notion, any comprehension of our precarious character, or the threat in our success.

For this, too, is the place where the swart vaquero, your buckaroo, once rode, with jingling spur and bit and *juaquima* and snake-like lariat. He, like the eternal sporting gentleman, wore his clothing as if it were color, purest desire, splashed on him. His trousers were laced together to the knee with bright ribbon run through eyelets and fastened with silver bell-buttons; he had a pink sash at his waist and a colorful serape over all. None of the comely bruins of that race ever gave these hombres the pumpkin.

At the end of the rodeo season, the middle of May, the "Matanza," the killing season, began. And so, from the Legislature of Drinks down would come riding that one fellow designated as the "Judge of the Plains" whose duty it was to inspect brands, stoop to catch the confession of each singed calf, arbitrate all disputes, create disputes where there were none, steal as many hooves as he could—for the sake of the Legislature's greasy union—and determine the number of cattle to be slaughtered. After the butchering, the hide was taken off the beast's wheezing corpse and dried; the tallow, fit for market, was forced into bags made from hides; the fattest portion of the meat was made into soap, while some of the best was cut, pulled into shreds, and dried in the sun. The rest was thrown to the dogs, thousands of which were kept to clean up after a matanza. It was the dogs, finally, who were the frailty in the vaquero's seamless logic of meat. The dogs gave the secret away. For even in those parts of the year distant from the matanza, blood clung to the vaquero's boot heel like memory. And so when he rode into town, tall and luminous, a string of the curs followed at his horse's heel. Urgent.

It was for this reason that no vaquero was allowed entrance to my gambling saloon. For the saloon was a splendid parlor, fitted up and decorated in glittering style. I grant you, we were dependent on the vaquero and blood, but we were blood's pure, transcendental Form. We couldn't be contaminated. We couldn't have the dogs howling in the parlor. And so even if the vaquero's gold was heaped in hillocks on the tables all around, even if his buxom woman—her brown pelt garbed in our gauds—was reclining in our love seats, he at our swinging door I stopped cold. Let him gawk. A protest I could meet with a little bullet between his black eyes. After all, there was no mercy. We occupied all the cushioned seats in all the synagogues. We were irrepressible.

Invocation: Oh you of supple mind. You immune to guile. Live like a madman, beyond all limits, go wherever you please. For the Others only live to die.

From the lonely date that coxswain John Gilroy and his comrade, Deaf Jimmy, deserted Her Britannic Majesty's ship, the good Man o' War, *Prodigious Duty*, and established themselves in San Ysidro, the Spaniards and their polluted descendants, the vaqueros, were doomed. The Alvarados, Castros, Martinezes, Sepulvedas, Estudillos, Moragas, Briones, Sunols, Sotos, the Peraltas, Altemeranos, Amadors, Mirandas, Berryessas, the Pachecos, Bacas, Alvisos and Naviagas—all these grand old families, each family under the rule of their kind old patriarch—all these rich, extravagant, confiding, simpleminded, oldfangled, dead people. Oh, perfidious England! You're no virus, but confronted by just one

60

issue of your cult, the happily dreaming Spanish legions were impotent, then irredeemable.

However, as the industrious Legislature of a Thousand Drinks sagely maintained, this business is complicated and needs deft handling. For there was a far term, a latter bracket on the Spanish destiny which was, as we are all too aware, the termination of the national amusement of that amiable people of cherished memory, the bullfight. In 1854 the Legislature passed "An Act to Prevent Noisy and Barbarous Amusements." Well, it happened that after the enactment became a law, a great preparation was made for a bullfight at the old Mission of San Juan Bautista. Those responsible were notified by officers that they must desist from the undertaking. The people then consulted Dr. Wiggins, friend to the sporting gentleman, and a man of genuine wit. He advised that prolific people, "They can do nothing with you. This is an act to prevent noisy and barbarous amusements. If they arrest you, you will be entitled to trial by jury; the jury will be Americans; they will, before they convict you, have to find three things; first, that a bullfight is noisy; this they will find against you; second, that it is barbarous; this they will find against you; *but an American jury will never find that it is an amusement in Christ's time.* Go on with your bullfights!"

One notices, however, that Dr. Wiggins did not get so carried away by his conviction that he joined that simple crowd. All I can observe is that the fathers and sons of that terminal race were arrested. It was reported that in effectless protest the wives and daughters came to the jail's gate draped in their fine silver pendants but draped as well with fresh strips of flesh from the loins of the bulls, hung across their shoulders like enormous tongues. But, fah!, there was nothing sound in their reasoning. Therefore, the last custom of a former civilization passed away.

As I said, I have lived my protracted life in this shed, in among the tules—the antithesis of my spangled career as your estimable professor of cards—as a courtesy, a kindness to all. For believe me, I do not jest, I am an abyss. Only the wanton boys who take the short cut to the public school know of me. They call me "Fart." And "Hey fuck you." They bang the ritual stones off the side of my crib. Some of the wiser of them—the little fellows, usually, who'll be betrayed in their turn—call me "Father Time." Now, there they have me. Because I did father time. I got time by a squaw, of bloodthirsty character, named Anistaba. I remember her head was covered with gashes, self-inflicted, which when I touched my lips to them sent steam into the very air. It's from that moment you may date our cosmos, gliding on its well-greased track.

So there's more danger in clearing this last patch of marsh, in creating a foundation for another suburb, than is easily seen. For when the job is done, I shall have to step forward, my various organs fastened like a soldier's medals to my jacket, and the good people of Noble Savage Court or Happy Hunting Condominiums will be given the understanding that their bodies are not solid like rubber; they, too, are implicated in Time's bloody spectacle.

When they gather round, when I see the childish faces of those telecommunications experts, those genies of the information industry, those silicon hotshots, and their impoverished families in too much pain to know how to feel it, I'll tell them this story.

□

Invocation: Oh, you who took the A train! You who praise Rapid Transit! You who think of Space and Time as impediments! Listen to the story which comes to you on this rat's breath. Mothers, tell your children! There is one vice common to you all, a love of the game!

Once upon a time. The story comes to me, now, as vivid as the sheets of newspaper, *The Oakland Tribune*, which the bay wind applies to the side of my shed. I remember a large, muscular female who sprang, quick as thought, upon the back of the Sheriff. I remember the red hand of murder. I remember a people among whom violent death ran. And I remember a wild-looking place, a lonesome locality, where many lawless characters prowled. And there, across the dusty street, was my own establishment, The Change of Heart Saloon, the original diamond in the rough. A shiny thing.

On the night I have in mind, I arrived at a gloomy hour on horseback. I came through the swinging door and saw that events had been waiting for me. They had need of my eyes. You may recall, this was the Chinese Year of the Pistol. January 19, 1877. Four men stood around my finest pool table. They'd been grinning and chalking their cues for several hours, awaiting my arrival. Behind each of them were bags of freshly minted coin. An outrageous scene! Flagrant as a skull through which the brain protrudes. But I was as cool as that sporting portion of the community I represented. I went behind the bar, poured a shot of whiskey and said to my barkeeper, "Mr. O'Brien, you may put down your shotgun," for he was a faithful, nervous son of Ireland, "I know these men."

And know them I did. One was that same Leon Castangau, by

name, of New Orleans. A Frenchman, expert at billiards, jovial and convivial, but he'd once killed a man by biting off his thumb. Then that most desperate hombre, Soto, wanted on some days for the murder of Ludovisci. He was large, powerful, with long black hair, large eyes of an undefinable color: an altogether tigerish aspect. Then, the biggest grinner of them all, a Chinaman, Low-Kee, who had once mutilated one of his fellow Celestials for reasons that were so narrow, so difficult of access that his bewildered jury was obliged for acquittal. And finally an Indian, Wampett, alias Figaro, a drunken, brawling, besotted fellow, of whom the less you know, the better.

They had the pool balls ready and racked. So, from beneath the counter I retrieved a small black box. I brought it to these gentlemen as if it were an engagement ring for my beloved. I opened it and there sitting like an enormous pearl was our peaceful cue ball. Humming a little tune I'd picked up from a Norwegian fellow, I placed the ball on the table. I expected someone to say, "Let the game begin." Instead, little Low-Kee himself said, "I'll have a man for my supper." It was that kind of night.

It was decided that these four gents would play a tidy game of eight-ball, Low-Kee and the Frenchman against Soto and Wampett, winners take all. Their host, the consistent Professor Silkman, deducted a modest charge for his services and blandishments. They drew cards for the break and Wampett chose the ace of clubs. Black but not necessarily deadly. He picked up the lucid cue ball daintily, and I noticed the grey earth beneath his nails. With a ferocious thrust he sent my pearl into the rack and the balls scuttled like sea creatures obliquely about the table. The eleven ball staggered to the corner pocket and collapsed into that space.

So Wampett kept his turn. He took a step back and chalked up. He faced his enemies and said, "Do you want to kill me?" "No," said Low-Kee. "Yes," said Castangau. Suddenly, the youthful French fiend slashed the unfortunate man in the face with a knife. A scuffle ensued and the Indian Wampett was stabbed in the left side. I ruled that Soto would be allowed to take up his partner's turn. Soto, the noxious, fatty perspiration standing on his face, stepped to the table, but not before placing his black revolver on the rail beside him, hammer cocked.

Although I was not at that moment, I ought to have been reminded of certain famous Resolutions of the Legislature of a Thousand Drinks. How often they admonished us of the uncertainties of life. How often they reminded us that the apparently solid self was only energy, only the sun's light through a crystal. All things, they were determined to show, are frail, are ever poised on the brink of collapse.

This insight might have been of great consolation to our sporting friends, Soto et. al., later in the evening when Castangau lay dead, a bullet from my own derringer imbedded in his forehead's boney plate, a bullet from Soto's enormous *pistola* at home in his belly. By that time Soto was only modestly better off. Blood spurted in a nice, even rhythm from his left wrist and he was obliged to take his messy shots with one hand. Only Low-Kee remained whole, but his smile was some degrees sickened by uncertainty. A wee half-hour later, Soto was drained and dead beneath the table, and Low-Kee was prostrate and bleeding himself, a scythe-blade in his hand, a scythe-blade wound frowning over the rim of his brow. Their game had reached this point: the eight ball clung to a whisper of felt, suspended above a side pocket. My motherly cue ball muttered to it, moments away, dead on.

Well, it was closing time, anyway.

So I took my walking cane—yes, the one given me by the noted desperado Tiburcio Vasquez—and, perching a slender hip on the table, drove the eight ball home. Backspin hopped the cue ball into its master's coat pocket. I then summoned Mr. O'Brien and had him collect the clutter of coin. Finally, to sad Low-Kee I came and peered into his sooty face.

"How now? Not dead yet, puppy? Hast thou still something of the quick about thee?"

A little bubble rose to his lips and, popping, said, "I win."

"Won, old mole? Yes, you take the prize, you do. Bless me if you don't."

Need I say that their bags of coin sat in the vault of my bank, next day, where for years they garnered dividends, financed speculations, underwrote ventures, and generally accreted, cell by cell, like a tumor?

Invocation: Oh you adventurous voyagers, you who spread yourselves over a country that seemed to suit your taste. You who cultivated farms, established vineyards, erected sawmills, then actually sawed the lumber, and did a thousand other things that seemed natural to you. You have manipulated the world and gained satisfaction. You have gouged chaos out and put an eyeball in its place.

I know that some of you may think that my story is the result of a disordered brain. No doubt, I am past my prime. But in my time I have been a leader, enticing young Californians up the broad trail concluding in distinction. I have practiced the seductive arts for the good of my kind. The rest of you can go hang.

Still, I am sorry to see the last of these wetlands, the last of these covering tules, join the dead. It reminds me that success is a form of loss. A form of disenchantment. The gorgeous feather tules, in my judgment, have helped soften this fact.

Now a fellow, one of my own blood, a native Californian, climbs down from his bulldozer. He points to me for his companions. They stop their enormous bug husks which, paused, rattle awkwardly. I rise, my legs thin like an egret's. The corner posts of my shed shiver with the damp and cold, and begin to collapse. This is the present past; it is deep time. The heavy machine operator approaches me timidly, a styrofoam cup of coffee, a vexed peace offering, outstretched. Sadly, I must report that the solicitous look of dead people is in his eyes. No doubt he'll wrap me in his own jacket, and seat me like a child in the cab of his monster. He'll offer me a glazed doughnut and a thermos of his violent java. That should get the heart rushing. Like in the old days. A hurricano, boys! Then I'll rise agitated as one of your hysterical sisters, voluminous as a demented house guest in whose head a vessel has popped. Out of that rupture will rush a dismal welter of memory. What a riot!

Then I'll start talking. And I'll tell everything I know.

History is the Debris of Duality

History is the debris of duality.

All those capable of valid cognition affirm this. However, even those of an empirical mind can be convinced. Consider the following experiment.

Remove the sandy soil from an area where it is suspected that a man has been freshly murdered. Put the soil in a basin of water. If in fact a man has been freshly murdered upon this soil, the water will exhibit a bloody color and a greasy scum will rise to the surface.

This division of blood and scum from water reveals the truth of what we contend about history. Still, some of you, those most thoroughly a part of the present delusion, may remain skeptical, may want to hear the story that goes with the soil and its fatty addendum. Here it is, for all the good it will do you.

This is from *History of Contra Costa County*, by J.P. Munro-Fraser, Historian, published by W.A. Slocum and Company, San Francisco, 1882.

"On November 16, 1872, one Valentine Eischler, a German, was killed on Marsh Creek, about eight miles southeast of Antioch, near what is called Chemisal. He was living with his wife upon a small farm, and had in his employ one Marshall Martin. During the stay of Martin, Mrs. Eischler formed a determination to get rid of her husband, and several plans were formed by her and Martin for carrying into effect her deadly purpose."

At the time of these events, in Antioch, wood was never painted. People were too depressed to paint things. It was difficult enough finding the resolve to build shacks to live in. Fine, powdery, light brown dirt was everywhere. It invaded the fabric of all Mrs. Eischler's cotton dresses. She lived in dirt, she wore dirt, wood was rough and full of splinters because no one painted it. You couldn't touch your own house. Also, people ate only meat because there were not yet any Japanese truck farmers and everyone was too sad to grow their own vegetables. They had no faith in things coming up out of the ground. So when they got hungry they simply killed something and ate it, unless they were very depressed in which case they found old meat and ate it. This made people sick in spirit and near suicide, but sex stood between them and death as a last hope. No, you can't call it hope. These were people with a desperate lust. This is what accounts for Marshall Martin's attraction to Mrs. Eischler. He saw her dirty cotton dress hanging on her fat thighs. They'd only known each other for twenty minutes and they were out in the barn humping each other clumsily, without craft, in a pile of straw that—I'm telling you—had some animal dung mixed in it. At any rate, meat has its own logic and its conclusion was that the husband, Valentine Eischler, had to die. Perhaps they wanted to have sex in a bed. I don't know.

"In pursuance of the plan, Martin went to Antioch one day and purchased a quantity of arsenic, and when he came home she mixed some of it with stewed pumpkin and put it upon the table for supper, but it so happened that Eischler did not partake of any of it."

But of course Eischler hated stewed pumpkin, as who shouldn't. This shows the depth of Mrs. Eischler's stupidity or madness. In addition, the pumpkins of that time were not better than our own, were not more natural because less a part of factory farming. They were runty things of a brown color that when ripe tasted of an old book which had been soaked in bad water and half dried. To top it all, Mrs. Eischler was incapable of keeping dirt—I mean clumps of dirt—out of the food she prepared. She saw it there, most often, but she was too sick at heart to do anything about it, to scoop the dirt out.

"The next morning it was thrown down the privy vault."

The Eischlers had to dig a new outhouse every six months because of the quantity of Mrs. Eischler's cooking that went into it, in addition to all of the poorly digested sinews of animals that they shat.

"A few days afterward she repeated the dish; but Martin claimed that he persuaded her to throw it away."

It was clear to Martin that no man would ever willingly eat Mrs. Eischler's pumpkin stew.

"She then wanted Martin to tell Eischler that there were some pigs for sale at Point of Timber, and to go along with him in the wagon, get him to drinking, and then buy a bottle of whiskey and put arsenic into it."

Martin had the little packet of arsenic in one hand and the whiskey in the other. They were bumping through the cold November night in Eischler's buckboard. But the mental connection that would allow Martin to know what the purpose was in killing Eischler failed to fire. He looked over at his employer, buried in his hat with his collar up against the chill, and suddenly got an erection. What did that mean? He got very confused and depressed. He wanted to drink the whiskey, but then he couldn't put the poison in it. He looked at the bottle and then the little packet then put the packet back into his coat pocket. He opened the whiskey and drank. It settled on the badly digesting pork loin in his stomach. That's all he had in his stomach, this cheap whiskey which didn't even have a label on the bottle, and the dead pig meat. He'd be even more depressed the next day and yet he'd wonder why.

"Another plan was then formed by which Martin was to knock Eischler off the wagon on the way home from Antioch, and run the wagon over his head."

How hard is it to run a wagon wheel over a man's head? I suspect it takes a lot of practice and a good working relationship with the team of horses. A lot of trust between the driver and the animals.

"A neighbor riding home with them prevented the execution of this plan."

Thanks for the ride! My pleasure. Say hello to the missus for me. I sure will. Tell her I'd appreciate it if she sent over some of that pumpkin stew she makes. I'll tell her.

"Then she suggested that Martin should shoot him."

Eischler was snoring in a chair beside the stove. Martin had taken his smelly penis out and was bumping Mrs. Eischler with it on the floor in front of her husband. Then she remembered that some people used guns when they committed murders.

"Martin had a revolver which he had purchased from a man who got it in Vallejo, and it would be necessary to go there to get cartridges to fit it."

Are we to understand that in those days if you bought a horse in Oakland you had to return to Oakland in order to buy hay whenever the horse wanted to eat? Or perhaps the make of the gun was a Vallejo Special.

"She gave him the money to go there, and he got the cartridges and returned."

The contempt she felt taking the soiled dollars bills from the coffee can. The hate she felt for this man who couldn't provide his own money for killing her husband. It made her want to hit him in the head with a rock. It made her want to pull up her green dress that was brown from filth and sit on his stupid dick and hit him in the face with a rock.

"The day upon which the murder was committed, Eischler went to Antioch for a load of flour. Martin accompanied him, according to instructions. Before starting she placed an old blanket in the wagon so that Martin, after killing Eischler, could wrap the body up in it, and when he returned she would go with him to an old well near by and they were to throw the body down the well, pour coal oil upon it and burn it up."

The amazement of the neighbors! The well was vomiting flame and it smelled like the plates of greasy duck, hunted easily in the abundant bay marshes, that they ate for dinner. They could hear the echoes from the screams of everything that had died to make room for them. In Antioch, in 1897, whenever the name of Chief Joseph was mentioned these echoes would mysteriously fill the air.

"Martin's heart failed him, and he did not shoot Eischler."

Martin put the revolver up to Eischler's temple, but when he looked at his victim's face one last time before pulling the trigger, he got confused. He couldn't remember what his own face looked like. It might look like that face. Maybe Eischler was about to shoot *him*! He dropped the gun with a cry. As it is with people who are going to die, Eischler noticed all this but forgot before he got around to picking up the gun. Martin sighed with relief.

"When they returned she was very angry with Martin for not carrying out her plan, and told him that he did not love her one bit or he would do as she wished him to. Martin says that while he was watering a cow...."

How like our own experience it is for Martin to decide at that moment, "I must water a cow."

"...Mrs. Eischler came out and commenced talking to her husband. They had some very high words; he heard Eischler say to his wife: 'Woman, take your clothes and go back to the w—house you came from.' Then Mrs. Eischler stepped back and picking up the ax, said: 'I'll give you w—house,' and struck her husband on the back of the head, knocking his body over a wagon-tongue so that his body doubled over it; she then straddled the tongue and struck him two more blows on the front part of the head."

A woman straddling the enormous tongue of wood, the ax above her head, the line of descent for the ax so well plotted, little dots in the air, the supine body of the husband, his head buzzing like a homing device for the blade of the ax.

"Then she called Martin to come and help her drag the body into the stable. After placing it in the stable Martin went to saddle his horse for the purpose of going to the Good Templars' Lodge, at Eden Plains School-house, about two miles away."

What is in this Martin's head? If it were a Tuesday, they'd be playing checkers at Good Templars'. He'd lose five or ten bucks for sure and everyone would wonder, "Where the hell is Martin's game tonight? He's usually more crafty than this."

"While fixing his horse, he says that she went into the stable with the ax and struck the victim two more blows, and that when she came back out she said that she had found him sitting up, but that she had fixed him now."

She had found her husband with three hatchet chops in his head sitting up. But she had fixed him now. With the ax again.

"When Martin returned from the Lodge she told him to go and arouse the neighbors and tell them that Eischler was dead in the stable, and that the horses had kicked him to death. He obeyed."

Oh come! Mr. Eischler is killed by horses! They'll have to be put down, now. We can't have murderous horses! That's bad meat!

"When the neighbors came some of them suspected that he had been murdered."

When they walked into the stable, they lost their balance, no one could stand up. So they knew there was a warp there. Then they saw Mrs. Eischler's bloody freckles.

"The next day when they went to examine the body they found a great many hoar-hound burrs upon the woolen shirt of the deceased, and by this means they found where the body had been dragged to the stable. Afterwards, they noticed the flies gathering upon Martin's shoes and pants...."

Martin felt awkward. Why was everyone looking at him? Why were they looking at his feet? He looked down and could hardly see his shoes so obscured were they with carrion loving flies, thick as flies. He wanted to scream but he forgot how. This is also something that has happened to you, I believe.

"...and this fact, together with the burrs upon the woolen shirt, led them to make search for the place where the murder had been committed. During this search Martin was very active in leading them off in different directions...."

Over here by this spotted dog, this is where it didn't happen. No, over here by this fig tree. He wasn't murdered here.

"...but finally they came to the wagon and examined the sandy soil around it. They soon found a damp place, and upon putting some of the sand in a basin of water it exhibited a bloody color, and a greasy scum rose to the surface."

The end.

This tale proves nothing. What support it gives to wrathful empiricists isn't worth the smell of the gas that erupted like clockwork from the flesh eaters we here describe. So ends our discussion of history as the polemical shards of our collective humiliation. Anyone who cares about such matters is an idiot.

Of course, anyone who fails to care about such matters is also an idiot.

"It is not proper that we should here note the shocking details of their executions; these will remain in the minds of many of our readers."

I, Loeit Langenbrucke, Knowing What I Know...

Dear Curt:

Sorry, brother, to learn in your last letter of your appalling situation. So, life is once again complex? Being myself only too recently relieved of similar complications, I observe your current trouble with a terror no whit uncertain. But perhaps my own recent escape from Love's ambiguous moan makes me the ideal person to console you in your present scrape. First, some completely worthless advice: quit your job. You professor types have this cotton candy parading by you at all hours. It would be unnatural for you not to WANT. (As for those who know nothing of "want," let them live with their corrupt desires.) Second, at least stop teaching Boccaccio. He turns teenagers into veritable philosophers of infidelity. So, you can stop that stuff!

Above all, remember that your magnificent obsession is trivial. Small making. You are now as ridiculous and diminished as that joker in Buñuel's *The Obscure Object of Desire* who buys his lover a house and then must watch from the wrong side of that house's gate as she goes down on Manuel or Pedro or who-the-fuck. One admits, though, his pain was exquisite.

Therefore, I envy you.

At any rate, your drama is pure opera. Plain excess. Which brings me to my real purpose in writing. I have a story to tell you which involves opera, involves in fact the great Caruso, in a situation which might—as you would say, Herr Doktor—deconstruct the apparent Necessity, Fate, Forward Propulsion of your liaison. For there is a gap in romance's flawless complexion, through which we might force a certain repressed, just as medical artisans of old obliged worms from wounds.

So, go, little letter, and sing in the ear of my friend what my IBM PC presently hums.

In March of 1906, during the first mad years of "Caruso fever," the Metropolitan Opera Company and its new star Enrico Caruso visited San Francisco as part of its national tour. They checked into the extravagant Palace Hotel for what was to be a two week season. But on just the second night—with the tenor's *Ridi, Pagliaccio* still resonating from the opera house, shocking the remainder of the city—there came the Great Quake, which destroyed that same opera house and caused fires which burned twenty-eight thousand buildings. (I wonder if anyone has ever bothered to investigate the effects of a voice as absolute as Caruso's on a fault as fragile as the San Andreas.)

Caruso was tossed from his bed by the force of the tremor. He had been dreaming that he was in a boat crossing the impetuous sea on his way home to bright Naples. His fall of course woke him, so he went to the window and threw up the shade and saw the city dissolving, flames already streaming up the sides of Victorians. And the following words occurred to him, "Fire is not fire; therefore, it is fire," which made him think he was going mad, so he called for his valet, Mario, put on a robe and went to the clamoring street below. Once there, he confided to his servant, "It is nothing."

Mario nodded.

Caruso continued as the masonry fell and the buildings toppled,

"In fact, Mario, anyone who reasons properly"—they were strolling toward Market Street, looking for a cab—"understands that when the world displays itself so insanely, in such obvious contradiction to its ordinary habits, one is not obliged to tolerate it (any more than one is obliged to tolerate the pretensions and affronts of a young man who thinks that he is the next *bel canto*). One may instead with good conscience remove oneself to a place where things are as they should be." (All of this, by the way, is in the *dolce stil* of their native tongue.) "In short, Mario, I propose we hie ourselves to the docks and, more to the point, the boats at the dock."

Mario grinned.

Needless to say, once they reached the docks, down by the Ferry Building, they discovered that they weren't the only ones who had considered that now was a good time to be somewhere other than San Francisco. There was a tyrannical crowd around the few boats and ferries. Police and soldiers tried to keep order, which meant forcing would-be refugees at revolver point back toward the flames where, it was clear to the soldiers, their true duty waited: fighting the enemy, brigand fire.

Perhaps it was Caruso's generally useless rotundity that kept the soldiers from forcing his enlistment, or perhaps it was the altogether silly-seeming tasseled tarboosh which he had placed on his head, or maybe it really was, as legend has it, the autographed photo of Teddy Roosevelt, the American president!, that allowed him to make his way to the boats. Not far from where he stood, the Metropolitan had finally found a launch to carry its singers to Oakland, but they couldn't wait any longer for Caruso. So he was forced to use what was at hand, a small tug-like boat used to carry fruit from the East Bay to the markets in San Francisco.

The boat's captain said, "Get on if you like, but I'm not going to Oakland. I'm going south to San Lorenzo."

Your own sweet home, Curt!

That actually sounded sort of homey to the Neapolitan as well, so he climbed aboard. As the boat pulled away, Caruso found the energy to turn back on the now super-luminous city and shake his fist. "I never come back here! Never!"

By the way, Curt, and this is apropos of absolutely nothing, has the news about the horrible sparrow blight in this part of the country reached darkling Illinois? It is an amazing, disgusting thing to see. I guess the facts are that local sparrow flocks have contracted a nasty disease of the claw. Ornithologists suspect that it is a bacterial infection which thrives under the crusty, fishy scales of their feet. But the awful consequence of it is that their little toes turn black and then detach in a very short period of time. You don't know how many tens of thousands of sparrows live about you until you find yourself in the yard raking up their bodies, forming piles of them at the curb for the big, municipal street sweepers. Of course, at first my cat thought it was all some wild happy dream, but now even she sits watching the bird-frenzy in cat-confusion. She wants no part of it. I hear this contagion is moving north. The sparrows themselves spread it miles in a day. They fly continually, since they cannot perch, fleeing what they can't help but not see: the terror of their own missing parts.

When Caruso arrived at Robert's Landing, what he saw elated him. For San Lorenzo Grove was in fact the garden paradise of

California, and he'd seen nothing like it since he left his sunny country. It was a place where San Francisco mothers brought their children to summer. Japanese gardeners tended to the truck gardens. Orange, pear and apricot trees were blossoming everywhere. And then, just a mile or so further inland, there was the Village of San Lorenzo and the Willows Hotel, which is where the captain suggested Caruso and his valet spend the next few days, until the opera company could be contacted.

Actually, the scene they found at the Willows was not a lot less confused than that which the fruit boat had fled. Here, though, it wasn't the hysteria of a crowd; rather, all chaos was focused in one selfsame person, Mrs. Alta Stroble, proprietress of the Willows. She was contending with two bits of disturbing information, one of which anyone would understand, the second of which said something about her particular proximity to the neurotic.

Mrs. Stroble had just learned that her husband had left for San Francisco to help fight the fires. At the same time she learned that the earthquake had cracked the Agnew State Mental Hospital out in the valley like an infested walnut and that hundreds of deranged patients were now loose. Mrs. Stroble saw them all—like a scene out of *Night of the Living Dead*—making a beeline for her. So she wept, trembled and screamed about death.

Up to this strode Caruso, a bit cynically, and asked, "May I be of some assistance?" The group around her parted not knowing who the dark stranger was, but sensing something of his greatness. He took Mrs. Stroble's hand and she quieted some. Then he spoke:

"I understand, Madam, your trouble. A tragic time has come to your beautiful home and your kind people. But you must resolve to survive! As we say in theater, *vesti la giubba*, the show must go on! We have our duties!"

He helped her gracefully to her feet, like Cavaradossi his Tosca, she staring at him in wonder. Caruso, however, being one of those men who could not meet a woman without conducting a silent poll—"Do I want to bed her?"— only wondered what fragrant stuffing she sat on. As she rose, he checked it out, brother.

"So, my dear lady, let me offer you a bargain. If you can resolve to return to your responsibilities—caring for those who, like myself, are temporarily without a home—I will provide for the entertainment of those here with songs and stories. For even in this harsh weather we must remember why we struggle to live: beauty, love, pleasure!"

The Agnew mental hobgoblins—rushing, their body parts flying off in all directions then recombining monstrously—were thus surprised to find themselves firmly seated and told to be quiet in the wings. For a master performer had come to claim stage center of Mrs. Stroble's consciousness.

Now, you know how these things go, Curt, that's why I'm telling this story to you. You're one of those who thinks that responsibility is a paradox. I mean, here Mrs. Stroble's husband is off risking his life fighting this epic fire, and she's looking over some hot Italian sausage. It's as if Penelope couldn't wait for Odysseus to get his butt out the door. And Caruso's no better. He's got a family, too, that he neglects. He ought to be saving his stuff for them, not out spreading his heat all over the place. Perhaps you would say, "That's folks for ya. Human nature strikes again." We'll see how long you can maintain that line.

What we know is that Alta Stroble did pull together and provide her new guests with food and warm rooms. To Caruso she gave the warmest room, very near her own. Oh, they were sly. How she trembled when the master paraded to the bath in just trousers, his suspenders over-arching his deep belly. And he's thinking to himself, "My God, I've got Vesuvius in my pants." They were hot for it, all right. But they'd make it even hotter by waiting a day.

So, the first morning they all had breakfast together—sausage, biscuits and gravy. Caruso thought about how nice Mrs. Stroble's bottom would look larded with this sauce. He'd like to lap it up. He'd pluck out the chunks with his teeth. Instead, he spoke to all the guests, in that sweet tenor which trembled or trilled in his excitement, "Let's adjourn to the garden for coffee after breakfast and we can talk, laugh, sing and tell stories until we hear that the nuisance in San Francisco is concluded. Later, I'm sure kind Mrs. Stroble's servants will be able to provide us fruit and wine. And so, my friends, to love!" And they all laughed and applauded.

I come now to a crucial moment in my story. Very recently, the Oakland, San Leandro and Hayward Railway had opened a spur off the main line down to the resort and picnic area in San Lorenzo. On Sundays, large crowds would take the electric cars to the grove to hear concerts performed by the 1st Regiment Band. Well, this railway line went right by the front gate of the Willows Hotel. And as Caruso, Mrs. Stroble and her guests sat in the garden on that pleasant March morning, an electric car pulled up in front and stopped in the middle of the track. The driver got out and began walking toward the gathering. On the car a passenger, too, got out in some anxiety and flagged down a car which happened to be passing in the other direction. The driver, a gloomy, slim man, dressed in a dark blue uniform and cap, came right up to Caruso and the rest and then sat down in one of the little iron garden chairs. But he didn't speak. Finally, Caruso himself addressed him.

"Do you bring us news?"

The man looked blackly at Caruso and replied, "Yes, of course.

82

My news is this: sooner or later all things return to nihility."

That shut 'em up for a moment. Already they were wondering if this guy was from the moon or what.

Caruso took a brave stance. "I am Enrico Caruso," he said.

"I am Loeit Langenbrucke."

Aha. So. Just right. They were getting nowhere with this dude. So Caruso tried irony.

"My friend, we've been sitting here in Mrs. Stroble's magnificent garden singing songs of old and telling stories in order to keep our minds off of the tragedy across the bay. Do you by chance have a story to tell us?" One or two foolish snickers.

But the driver took him seriously. He darkened, glowered and said, "I, Loeit Langenbrucke, knowing what I know, having seen what I have seen in San Lorenzo can surely tell you a story." He said so and turned his stare on Mrs. Stroble, who—yeah, you're right— was pale as death.

Then, of course, no one was real sure they wanted to hear this story, but they were afraid to leave, too.

"When I came to this place from my home in Rinekirick, Bairen, Germany, I was a fine, innocent young man. I had no vicious habits. And then I got my job with the railway, gliding on the multiple, lisping rails south and north in California's flawless weather. I was happy. And Mrs. Stroble here often allowed me to sleep in one of her rooms when the weather turned livid—no doubt the very room you sleep in, Mr. Caruso, to judge by the firm look of you. But you, too, are new to this California. Protect yourself, I say! Look to it! Latch your door at night! This is a foul people!"

Caruso glanced at Mrs. Stroble and it appeared she was about to cry. Of course, if her husband had been here, he'd have given this Langenbrucke lout a good knocking. Caruso was about to act in the husband's place when he suddenly imagined himself acting in the husband's place in another sense, you know, dipping another man's doughnut in his tea, and that made him self-conscious enough that he did nothing at all.

"Yes, Mr. Caruso, you would be wise to remain in your seat. Let me ask you, did you dream last night? Did you have any particular dreams? Because I will never forget the dream I had on just my first night in Mrs. Stroble's privileged room. In my country, my friends, we still believe in vampires, those for whom death is not death. So we lock our doors at night. But what reason in the world had I to fear a vampire here in San Lorenzo, reality's settled belly? None, until my dream revealed that Mrs. Stroble and her husband were not what they appeared to be. That nothing in San Lorenzo was what it appeared to be. There are corners in this town where the veneer has warped and you may peel it back if you are brave and then what splendid creatures you'll see! They're alive while all the rest of the world is sleeping! They're breathing!

"But I must continue my story. I must hurry. In my dream I was able to see into the bedroom of the husband and wife. Oh a nice conjugal scene, to be sure. There they were in their bed together, doing…aah!…things! And then her voice calling to me, 'Loeit! Loeit! Open your door!' And I do believe I would have opened the door except I stumbled in my sleep against a table and knocked over the water pitcher, crash! And then in the silence which followed I heard her cleverly slippered feet scuttling back to her shameful den."

Believe it, this story was doing a job on Caruso and the rest. You and I may see in it the origin of the willies, the heebie-jeebies, and the jim-jams. And Langenbrucke wasn't half done.

"Early the next morning, before returning to my responsibilities with the railroad, I took a walk down by the bay to clear my head. A beautiful piece of water if you can ignore the corruption at the

84

water's edge. And if you can ignore that, how corrupt are you? It was then I saw Them moving in the tidal dreck. Flotsam with lungs they looked like. A fool, I picked one up and rinsed away some of the filth in a pool and that's how I found their secret. It was the size and shape of an arm from a ceramic baby doll, only it was flesh, I tell you, and covered with fine, pale scales—as on a carp. And there were thousands of them twitching in the mud and gore."

At about this point in Langenbrucke's talk, in the distance behind him, another trolley pulled up behind his own and two men got out. They looked around, pointed in the direction of Langenbrucke and our storytellers, and then began walking toward them.

"Well, as you may imagine, I lost no time in leaving this Willows Hotel. I was terrified. But simple distance did me no good. My dreams were contaminated by this place. I dreamed that night that I was sleeping in Mrs. Stroble's poisoned lair"—he got up suddenly as if to reach across and strike the lady—"and I was waked by a scratching sound outside my window. I got up and went outside and saw that the sound was coming from the cellar door just beneath my window."

Now the two men from the trolley had nearly arrived.

"I pulled open the hatch door. At first, it merely appeared that the bay itself was under the house. Unguent, oozing, parasitic. But as my eyes adjusted, it became clear to me that it might be the stuff of the bay, but it was in no way original, natural stuff. It was made of clots of hair and blood and limbs from dolls, even doll eyes sparkling lugubriously, and the slime of fish. It was cresting and its tide knocked against the cellar door."

"All right, Langenbrucke, that's enough. Come along now." The men had arrived and, one on each side, had taken his arms. Caruso was on his feet, too, backing away from this portentous vision.

85

CURTIS WHITE

"But I'm not done with my story!" With a stunning shirk of his suddenly powerful arms, Langenbrucke freed himself. "I have something to show these people. I have brought some of it back from my dream." Now, a little paper bag appeared—like the sort of thing you'd put your lunch in—its bottom saturated with something fatty.

"I don't think these nice folks want to see what you have in the bag, Loeit, so just do what we ask, now." They shook him so that the sack fell and splatted on the ground like a pound of calves liver.

"The loon has probably been storing old mice in there," one of the men surmised for the benefit of the guests.

"But wait," Langenbrucke resisted, "I must tell them one more thing, they may still not believe me. If you don't believe me—especially you my great, fat wonder—and you won't peek in the bag, then go look under the hatch for yourselves. See, it's right over there."

They turned and, sure enough, there was a wooden hatch up next to the hotel, painted a lurid red.

"Go, open the hatch, see for yourselves, if you dare. Let forth those pieces, unless you fear how, once in your air, they will recombine. Think of the possibilities!"

And then, really, that was enough of that, they pulled him away. Back to work.

"What are you doing? Where are you taking me? I was just telling them a story. They asked me to. A good one, wasn't it? Bet I scared the pants off you. Tell these fools that we were just swapping tales, as you say. Please! I don't want to drive the little trains anymore!"

Well, Curt, you can imagine the state this left Caruso, the fragile Mrs. Alta Stroble and her guests in. First the earthquake, now this lunacy. But it was clearly Caruso who was most upset, perhaps because all of his expectations and understandings had been betrayed. He looked immediately to Mrs. Stroble for clarification, for reassurance. But that ample matron was so shocked that even if she had wanted to, even if she had known how, she would not have been able to deny what Langenbrucke had said. And that inability, I'm afraid, scared Caruso more than anything. It was time for him to run away.

"Well, I'm very tired and I seem to be coming down with a headache, so if you don't mind, if you will all excuse me, I think I'll return to my room." So said the worried Caruso. But he had no intention of staying in San Lorenzo for another moment. It was the Village of the Damned as far as he was concerned. So he grabbed Mario and the photo of Teddy Roosevelt and—thankful for once that he had no suitcase—fled out a back door. He'd walk the two miles to the dock and escape his earlier escape back to the flaming City. The fire seemed an easy thing to him now. He might even toss a bucket of water in its direction.

Fortunately, there was a small boat at the dock which he was able to hire for immediate departure. His stay in San Lorenzo was over, this brief episode in his illustrious life concluded except for one detail. As he struggled to board the little boat, he lost his balance and one foot plunged back into the bay where it was sucked up by the voracious mud. "My god, they have me this time! I'm a dead man!" The boat's skipper didn't see it quite so fatally. He grabbed Caruso's leg, gave it a yank and with a messy "splash" his foot was returned to him. His foot, but not his shoe. And as the boat drifted out toward deeper water, Caruso's shoe was left behind, sticking up like someone's ankle, half ingested by ages of decomposing sea life. He was still screaming when they docked at Fort Mason.

So that's it, Curt. Feel better? Did that clarify things? I'm sure you'll let me know. By the bye, if you're really committed to adulterous ways, there's someone down here I can set you up with.

I let her read your stuff and she is, shall we say, intrigued. She works in the typing pool here. Amazing to think she can do fifty words a minute with her toes! In my opinion, the miracle of the eighties isn't the microchip, it's special education. At any rate, as Mick Jagger says, "She's just dyin' to meetchooo."

All Best,

Blood Will Tell

You drank coffee at a counter. It was a B street cafe and it was about 9:30 in the morning. You sat at the end stool near the door, and a small package was beside your cup. You wore a red coat and a green sweater. You are about twenty-five years old and you wore your hair in an upsweep. Call *The Daily Didactic* if you recognize yourself, because you have won the Daily Dollar!

Doris, any chance we can get up a little earlier and just have coffee at home from now on? Because that cafe is getting to me. I haven't told you what happened there this morning. It's not just the coffee, although that's horrible. The people there are disgusting. So, I'm sitting there drinking my coffee and this guy turns to me and starts talking about wrathful deities. There was snot all over his face and he smelled like Thunderbird sauterne.

He says, "If someone has received the highest empowerment, he is permitted to practice in the wrathful manner." Then he grabs up a fork and growls at me. I thought he was going to stick me. My skin felt all bloated like I was his sausage or something.

Doris, what's so damned interesting in the paper? Put it down for a minute, I'm talking to you.

Dr. Paul S. Taylor, professor of economics at the University of California, Berkeley, sat in the auditorium of the Oakland Public Library listening to the chief librarian introduce him to a lecture hall full of farmers, veterans, newspaper reporters and just a few friends. He felt ill. He hated public speaking, but he especially hated to think that those he addressed might disagree with him. Or, worse yet, might find him personally repulsive. He had to speak on a very controversial topic that night: the economic effects of the return of Japanese farmers and laborers from detention camps to the east. He suddenly anticipated that his nose would begin to run when he spoke and that he would have to sniff, his sniffs echoing through the PA system. No, worse, it was blood. He was hemorrhaging. His brain was bleeding postnasally. Soon, people would know that his head was full of loose blood and that it leaked down through his nose when he stood and talked.

"And so it gives me great pleasure to introduce to you a very distinguished professor and concerned citizen. I'm sure he will have much to say to enlighten us. Dr. Paul S. Taylor."

Taylor went to the microphone. "Returning Japanese-Americans will not threaten West Coast farmers," he began.

Some buzzing out there. Like you see in movies about the labor movement or vigilantes outside the jail house.

"Japanese-American farm people do not breed like rabbits."

"God damn it! That's a god damn lie! I've seen 'em with my own eyes!"

There was hissing and shouting about egghead professors and then everybody left.

Most historians of the era use this event to mark the beginning of the worst period in postwar relations between whites and Japanese in the Bay Area.

Don and Doris went to a movie one night. *Kiss the Blood Off My Hands* was playing in downtown Hayward. Terrific movie. Film noir. Really made them feel alive. As they walked home they saw a group of four high school kids walking on the other side of the street. Three boys and a girl.

"Say," said Don, "Isn't it sort of late for these kids to be out on a school night?"

"I'll say," replied Doris. "What are their parents thinking about?"

The kids were standing in front of a house two blocks west of the Green Shutter on B Street. One of the boys ran up to the house, then returned to the group with two wire racks holding a dozen milk bottles, six in each. Then with a flash of panic, exhilaration, doom, and glee, the four hurled the twelve—three each—at the front door of the house. The bottles seemed to lunge through the air, accelerating in a way that intro to physics would never quite sufficiently explain. They were like brittle protoplasmic bags of light.

That's how it looked to Don. The porch light on the oblong bottles made it look like they were hurling radioactive sea creatures. He was stunned by the glamour of the spectacle. So violent. So true.

Doris was appalled by his reaction. She showed him the newspaper headline the next day. BOYS HELD IN MILK BOTTLE BOMBARDMENT. "Bombardment, Don. Someone could have been hurt."

"But Doris, that doesn't matter if the gesture was beautiful."

91

Margaret Steno stood at Hesperian and Paseo Grande and thought: "This is my chance." She was fourteen and, as her mother would later report to the police and *The Daily Didactic*, "she liked to hang around dance halls." Her mother had given her twelve dollars for groceries and postage stamps. But Margaret's quick arithmetic demonstrated to her that with twelve dollars she could catch a bus to San Francisco and still have ten seventy-five left, to start her new life. She thought that was all she'd need. Well, her mother never heard from her again. So, Margaret must have been right about that ten seventy-five.

"If military control over civilians is a tolerable response to crisis situations, we might as well declare in favor of a modern police state patterned after the Visigoth code."
—Letter to the Editor, *The Daily Didactic*, 1947

One of the most notorious cases of anti-Japanese harassment after the war was that of Summio Doi. Summio Doi was a fruit rancher in Placerville, California. When he returned from the Japanese internment camp at Manzanar in 1946, he was keenly resented. Actually, he was fortunate to have something to return to. Most of the Japanese on the Coast had been forced to sell all of their property and businesses, usually at about twenty-five percent of market value. But Doi had refused to sell. That left him somewhat better off than those who had been given bus tickets to Chicago and nineteen dollars. Of course, after four years of neglect, his orchard was in much need of repair. But he was free!

Soon after his return, a local farmer emptied a shotgun into a window of Doi's house. At the trial the gunman was congratulated for not using a more deadly .44 rifle and was given a suspended sentence.

At that point Governor Earl Warren (who was, in fact, the California politician most responsible for the creation of the camps back in 1941-42) and his Attorney General, Robert Kenny, stepped in. Kenny said, "There is no open season on Japanese in California."

"They are too clever, industrious, thrifty and prolific. Their swarming children, their natural clannishness, their inevitable loyalty to the Japanese empire, their swarming children. This is what I mean by 'rising tide.'"

—Lafcadio Hearn

You are a blonde-haired young woman who sat in a downtown office building this morning over a drawing board. A young man entered and handed you a stack of papers. You said you were expecting the papers and thanked him.

He left your office, got into a green sedan, bought a hamburger on East 14th and drove to the Plunge to eat. While there, he nursed a magnificent erection out from his flannel trousers. You really caught his eye! But because this was only the first time he'd seen you, it must be said that your image and Lana Turner's were indistinguishable.

If you recognize yourself....

Dr. Paul Taylor was asked to serve on the committee organized to produce the "Japanese-American Evacuation and Resettlement Study." The committee met in Sproul Hall on the Berkeley campus. Taylor sat at the long table. The thickness of the varnish over the wood depressed him. But everything depressed him. After all, as he saw it, the whole current coastal racial crisis followed from his one pathetic evening of ineptitude and failure. A colleague had referred to his speech as "the contradictory catalyst for an unprecedented wave of bigotry." He was losing weight; he was driving his wife to drink, wear party dresses, and visit the night spots in North Beach. But he couldn't get an image out of his mind, a billboard: "The Sons of the Golden West say, 'Keep California White.'"

"But why white? What is the real form of 'white'? It's only because the attainment of whiteness is false that it can be achieved at all. Isn't that right?" he asked his colleagues. They weren't very patient with him and asked if he'd like to be relieved of his responsibilities.

He really was very depressed. He was going to kill himself if this kept up.

A television is drawing people together in the Village. The home of Mr. and Mrs. Cecil Turner on Via Cielo has become a popular meeting place now that the Turners own an RCA television. Five nights a week they entertain twenty-five or more people.

"You should see it," says Mrs. Turner, "It's wonderful. The floor is covered with children.

"The other night, I couldn't help it, I just threw myself down among them and rolled around. And they lifted me and passed me over their heads. It was like being embraced by a mob of tiny creatures. How wonderful it felt."

Hockey games and roller derby are among the most popular shows watched by the Turner's grateful guests in their generous house.

I remember Terry Naruo. (I haven't thought of her in years. Terry, is the ether twanging about you now? Are your "ears burning"?) She was one of less than a half-dozen Japanese-American students at San Lorenzo High School in 1969. I remember being near her once when the relocation camps were mentioned. Her parents had been in a camp. She went quickly from her usual cheerfulness to sudden resentment.

"I can't believe people would do that," she said, looking at me with a killing distrust, as if to imply, "that you would do that to me." And, of course, she was right. I had done it. It was me the whole time!

One of the funny things about growing up in San Lorenzo was that it felt like we were growing up in a classless and raceless society. So much so that "class" and "race" meant almost nothing to us. The idea of a "rich" person was like a rumor. Where were they? What could they do with their money? We all owned a car and TV. How many cars and TVs could you want? And there were so few blacks or Asians that it was easy to think of them as "white like me."

Anyhow, I found out in our senior year that Terry had a crush

95

on me. I never acted on that knowledge. And now I urgently want to be able to go back and fuck with her. But I want to be able to go back and fuck with all of the women I might have fucked with but didn't. That's because I'm a hetero-masculinist who imagines that the Final Accounting will have to do with the varieties of sexual experience. Lord I was dumb. And I'm still that dumb.

A more generous way of looking at my present desire is that I now understand our separate histories, our conjoined situation, and our similar fates in a way that makes me care about Terry as I couldn't then. Still, I've never understood the compassion in sisterly/brotherly hugs. It's not enough. I never get it. "That's nice, but fuck me, then I'll understand." I feel like one of Kathy Acker's characters. I feel mutilated.

Terry, what parts of you are left and where are they? I'd like to get in touch.

It wasn't just that Summio Doi was Japanese. That wasn't the only reason that the people of Placerville—"Hangtown"—resented him. He offended in other ways. For one, he was an unapologetic "No-No Boy." When the Feds brought their questionnaires to the camps, they asked: would you serve in the army? Will you disavow all loyalty to the Emperor? But Doi's response was, "Why do they want us to serve when they consider us to be disloyal? I'm not going to do anything to go into the United States Army until the United States Government does something to remedy this unjust situation. So I say, 'No-No, just shove it up your ass.'"

Doi was also a Buddhist. And when he was asked about his situation and his persecutions past and present, he would often reply obliquely, in an "inscrutable" manner, since he was sure no one cared to understand him no matter what he said.

"Black Ishvara dwells in your land. He has great power, but his miracles are contaminated. He can give you increase in wealth, but only at the cost of false knowledge of yourself. He gives you a mind of self-grasping. You will not halt your suffering—even if you do not know your suffering as suffering—until you attain the path of seeing. Unfortunately, my suffering, too, will not cease until you attain the path of seeing."

Man alive, that ticked a bunch of them off all right.

"Be careful to differentiate between races. The Chinese and Koreans both hate the Japs more than we do. Be sure of nationality before you are rude to anybody."

—Lafcadio Hearn

In subsequent years, Don became a philosopher of beauty. Doris divorced him and he was fired from his job with the East Bay Municipal Utility District, but he didn't give a damn. He was a man who had seen things that made him wonder. Always he remembered, as a variety of mystical vision, the radiant milk bottles, their explosive trajectory, their truth.

He stayed home a lot, assembling model fighter planes. Then one day he read the following article in *The Daily Didactic*.

Japanese Farmer Dynamited

PLACER—Summio Doi, a local fruit rancher recently returned from the Manzanar Internment Camp, had his work shed dynamited late yesterday evening.

Local officials have arrested Elmer Johnson of the Anti-Japanese Citizens Committee. Johnson, it happens, is an AWOL soldier from Camp John.

Suddenly, it was all clear. Don saw the sticks of dynamite lunging through the air. He saw the brilliant explosion. The perfect shards of the shed, jagged and heartbreaking. He would go to this place, Placer.

Professor of Economics Hangs Self

You drove out of town in a '36 Studebaker. You were excited and in good spirits. You sang the Burma Shave signs aloud and laughed. You stopped at a Big Orange and had lunch. The valley was hot and auspicious.

When you drove past Summio Doi's shed, you stopped the car, got out and danced an inept jig. This was really the place! When you got to his house, only a bit further up a steep dirt road, you got out again. Another dance. The pineapple dance. You were tossing a pineapple from hand to hand. Where did you get that? You can't buy those at army surplus, can you? Even we are astonished.

Finally, you lob the pineapple in the living room window and, yes, it's really something. Glass and plaster and lathing come shredding back at you. You're so involved! You feel the cuts leaking down your face.

But when you go up to knock on the front door, we begin to

wonder if you know what the heck you're doing. No answer. Come on, somebody be home. Then you notice that something has been leaking out from beneath the door. You're standing in it. It's blood and it's really pouring out now. It scares you.

So you run away, but it seems to be flowing right after you. The dike has broken, Buster. You get in the car and try to start it but it's flooded. Nice job! Your carburetor is puddled with blood. So you run, back down the long dusty road, your foot prints a glaring scarlet behind you.

If you recognize yourself....

Terry! I know! Let's get down with the children in front of the TV and roll around! Let's put on our Mighty Mouse tee-shirts and watch the Flubadub cut up with the Doody man! Let's hug all the kids! C'mere, give me a big wet kiss.

Ex-prisoner of Japs is Killed Here

HAYWARD—Al Vislan, Hayward, was killed yesterday when his hot rod 1929 Pierce Arrow skidded, went up an embankment and overturned. He had driven into the hills behind Hayward High School to spin doughnuts with his brothers.

Vislan had been a prisoner of war on Formosa until 1946. He was discharged from the army only a week before this accident.

Local officials blame the incident on wrathful deities.

The Birth of Tragedy

Oh plausible, vicious reader, you gossip. "*Si può?*—May I address you?" I have a story for your contemplation which is in all ways false. In it, a genius of real estate, a colossus among housing contractors is depicted in the extremes of human misery. You will witness his passion, his rage and anguish, his bitter laughter. But do not concern yourself, for his tears are unreal. He is a puppet, some baggage. However, in one respect this tale allows a rudimentary truth: the suburb is the home of tragedy. And, I would suggest to you, if the suburb is the space within which the tragic has unfolded, may it not also be the origin of our ultimate ecstasy and salvation?

Come then! Let us begin!

Where David Bohannon was born and raised is not known. No historian—and no sensible person—has ever cared. Not cared because there was no reason or room for caring about the past of a man who had made denying the past the everyday principle of his life. He was far more concerned with a superb destination. Of course, there was a time when we assumed that Bohannon was created so that we could attend a junior high school named after him. But it is more than clear to me now that his purpose was much broader than that. He is one of those few who realized a bountiful vision of the future in his own lifetime. In fact, in a matter of months. In fact, at the rate of a vision every forty-five minutes.

"Every lot a garden spot" was the slogan for his practical, premature paradise.

During the war years, 1940-45, two-hundred-thousand workers and their families arrived in the San Francisco area. After the war, nobody left and others continued to pile in. We saw a tolltaker on the Bay Bridge weep in bewilderment and guilt, as if in some way he were responsible for the faithless crush. In the Tenderloin, beds never had a chance to cool because they were occupied the clock 'round by rotating sleepers. Chinese men sold interests in a cot or bed from laundry doorways to bleary Vets. The Negro Problem and the Coolie Nuisance were contained through the use of tiers of beds hooked four or five to a wall, Pullman style.

Fortunately, there was one among us with the capacity to imagine a cure for this homelessness. Dave Bohannon—master salesman, six-foot, strapping—created in the insistent sunshine the "California Method." He studied a model house and broke the manufacturing process into a series of standardized steps. He counted the number of pieces of lumber that go into a house, numbered each piece and precut it. The pieces were then preassembled into frames and wall panels on jig tables, which reduced carpentry to a matter of driving nails.

"This is a hammer and these are nails," Bohannon said to his employees.

The panels, enough for one house, were loaded on a truck and hauled to a concrete foundation. So, our Village began as an over-large assembly line. Bohannon used the precise scheduling of factory-production men. Bathtubs, shingles, doorknobs were at the appointed spot in the line when workers were ready for them. And in this way, an orchard of apricot and orange trees was translated into a community of homes, supermarkets, firehouses and recreation halls at the rate of a completed house in less than an hour.

Thus, the birth of our San Lorenzo Village. By 1947, it was done. Bohannon lived in it like a man in privileged dreams. He had arranged with duplicitous fate to allow a flood of beauty in his life. That is, it was this way until the Discovery of Doubt, Beauty's kissing cousin. On a cool, overcast evening in December of 1947, Bohannon finished a lonely cocktail at Pland's Villa (where the Leilani Sisters, "a pair of Hawaiian cuties," danced the native hula), then he walked across Hesperian Boulevard to the Lorenzo Theater. Perhaps this was also the evening of the Discovery of Bourbon, for furious motorists seemed to scream at him as they passed, as if he were some drunk. He was disoriented. Imagine, feeling alienated within your own achieved dream! But the unhappy fact is that earlier in the day he had looked upon his suburb—every sycamore in place, every lot a garden spot—and found it lacking. "That is not it," he said. "That is not what I had in mind." Now his sure reality seemed a hallucination. Lines of children for the Kiddee Matinee seemed to appear and disappear. A blimp-like image of Howdy Doody floated above the theater's enormous art deco tower which itself leaned like a threatening tube of Ipana toothpaste.

Bohannon fell toward the ticket booth and bought a seat in the loges for fifty cents. "Dark Mirror," starring Olivia de Havilland. In the lobby the average little men of this vet village were dressed in tuxedoes. They winked at him like Rocky Marciano. Fluorescent wall paintings of black leopards and Punjab boys in pajamas encouraged him to puke.

What we are discovering, hollow reader, is simply that Dave Bohannon lived in his creation alone. These were the effects of a terrible loneliness. Perhaps he had forgotten to make one of the little cottage homes for himself. What a dumb mistake!

Up in his balcony seat, it's quiet and frightening. Below him the darkness seethes. Frequently a popcorn box—flattened into a flying disk—soars across the movie screen like an enormous bat. His trousers are open and he grips his cock with certainty. It's not as comforting as being hugged by his mother, but she's gone and he's in his own world now and this handful of himself makes him less afraid.

Around midnight, after the third showing of *Dark Mirror*, we fear that Bohannon will be mistaken for a vagrant. Fortunately, the usher knows him.

"You'll have to leave now, Mr. Bohannon. We're closing for the night."

He waits patiently as Dave puts away his penis and gets to his feet.

"Tod," says Dave addressing the usher. "One hundred years ago, this land was occupied by the Digger Indians. They lived in filthy grass huts. When the smell of one got too bad, why, they just burned it down and built another. I don't call that pretty, do you?"

"No sir."

"Thank you, Tod."

Then he left the Lorenzo Theater and walked north on Hesperian, past the new sporting goods store, Bo-Bo's hamburger stand, and the fire station. He let himself into the Camp Fire Girl cabin at the Recreation Center, curled up in the center of a vivid, braided area rug and fell asleep.

His dream of Wanda.

David Bohannon has keys that will allow him into every house and building in San Lorenzo. But what he would really like is to be

103

able to use the key that would allow him into the house of Wanda, San Lorenzo May Queen of 1946. What he would like is to be able to live in Wanda's home. Because, to be frank with you, loitering in the theater and sleeping in the Camp Fire Girl cabin is not his idea of a friendly life. More important than that, he feels he loves her. But there is a problem: Wanda already allows a man to live in her home, her husband Roy.

So, for the present, David may only dream of her. In his redundant dream she emerges from her kitchen in the violent air, the screen door banging behind, and she arranges a green visor (yes, like that of a Reno sharpie) on her platinum hair. Then she slips out of her brief terry cloth robe and reclines in a redwood lounge for an afternoon of sun bathing. But in Bohannon's dream the gesture of robe shirking is redone endlessly—like a repeated loop from a home movie—until one can see that the fabric wears thin and frays at the seams. Sweet, tawdry revelation!

At the theater the villagers are watching *The Postman Always Rings Twice*. The criminally innocent husband has just left the drifter and his wife alone again. They do amazing things on a formica counter.

Roy rises from his seat beside undeniable Wanda and says, "That man, friends, is a fool and he gets what he deserves."

But a pure joker gives him the business: "Careful, Roy, who knows what kind of guy stays behind when you drive to the city every morning."

"Eh! What!—You think so?"

"Could be young Tod there. I swear he touched Wanda's elbow as he seated you. And I believe he could do a man's job. He's going out for football. Maybe he likes older women."

Roy smiles, wags his finger at blushing Tod, and replies, "Such a game, well, I'll give it to you straight, it would be better not to play it on me, neighbors. For these Hollywood pictures and life are completely different."

"Shut up and watch the movie!"

"Just a minute and I'm done. For if Wanda here I should ever surprise, you take my word, that's a moment were better not to come."

The villagers are puzzled by this display of passion, this unseemly promise of violence, and ask if he is serious.

"You're acting like a wop, Roy."

With a grand effort to control his temper, he says, "Me? Not me! I love my wife," and thereupon he gives her a peck on the cheek.

Wanda understands what this is about, what her husband's black expression augurs, but she says, "He's so silly. I don't know what he means by all this."

"I'm going to get the manager if you birds don't can it."

Roy sits down again and puts his arm around Wanda's shoulder. The neighbors say, "See? It was nothing. Everything's fine," and their attention returns to the movie. But not before Wanda glances with terror and longing up into the dark, pricey reaches of the balcony where sits David Bohannon, among the many empty seats only he can afford, a stranglehold on his crotch.

For the case had earlier become—see if you can follow this, clinging reader—that Bohannon had fantasized his union with Wanda so often and so fervently, had imagined his cock represented for her fond attention as real as the laminated mahogany leg

105

on her dining room table, that fantasy's far side had become the quotidian's near side, and on one unpredictable afternoon he had actually joined her in her bedroom and—you'll get this—had fucked her in Roy's bed, the smell of Roy's pomade on the pillows. You see, San Lorenzo was meant to be the kind of place where your dreams come true: a little place you can call your own and now true sex.

Afterwards, Wanda smoked one of those Tareytons with the charcoal filter, looked out the window and saw a house sparrow perched on the power line bringing the juice into her home. She said, "Oh, you birds! Flying so freely! Darting around in the streetless sky like birds! Where are you going?" She turned to David. "Perhaps to a distant land. Do you think so, David?"

"Yes."

"Perhaps to a distant country. The land of their dreams. Oh, can we go there, David?"

"Yes, sweetheart."

"To a village better than this."

"Better than this? You mean better than San Lorenzo?"

"Yes. Of course, better than San Lorenzo."

You may recall that in the corridor outside the main office of David D. Bohannon Junior High School there is a portrait of Bohannon. Curiously, we have never been able to look at this portrait without recognizing there Walt Disney. I mean, they really did look a lot alike, right down to that prissy little mustache. In fact, at age twelve, I didn't know it was Bohannon, I thought it was Disney. And it never for a moment seemed to me strange that Walt Disney's picture should be hanging in our school. Why not? The portrait implied a connection between Disneyland and San Lorenzo that seemed to me natural. But whatever there was "Goofy" about San Lorenzo was certainly well hidden. It was a kind of riddle, a first mystery for me.

Once, in the course of his daily, furtive wandering, Bohannon himself happened by the portrait. Of course, he can be excused for not recognizing himself. When would he have had the opportunity to look upon his own features? So, Bohannon too perceived there our pleasant, universal Uncle. He laughed to himself remembering the Disney cartoon in which that rapscallion Donald Duck destroys his entire house in order to kill a fly which had disturbed his otherwise flawless domestic ease. Then, with a frown, he realized that he understood exactly how the Duck felt.

It's plain to see that Bohannon's problem is simply that in spite of the fabulous opportunity he has had to create his own world, his completed creation still seems to him inauthentic. Lacking. Now, many another Developer would have been happy enough with the inauthentic, particularly in view of the profit that a forced inauthenticity would have provided him. Everybody going to work and paying him rent, hi-ho! It is thus to our David's credit that he was troubled and sought to find and develop what his Village was lacking. A sort of personal and community restitution perhaps. His first impulse was—dangerous as it would become—to eroticize the situation. Many another person has discovered that that indeed is one way of shakin' it up—for good and bad.

"O Wanda, your little window, dear undo!"

Yes indeed, shake it up baby! But this might as well be a hundred years before the Righteous Brothers, so he's just humming

"Something's Gotta Give."

Bohannon has been thinking about his problem in these terms: Wanda wants to run away to a dream-place where they can be eternally happy and yatta-yatta. Dave sees the folly of this but is afraid that pointing it out will lead to a general realistic assessment of what they're doing, in which case he too might be sacrificed in common sense's new reign. All he wants is to stay in San Lorenzo and yet have Wanda. Is that so never-never-ish? Does that make him fantasy's feeb? Being an inventive man, he has come up with a plan.

Last week, he had one of his crews raise a single house out in the new Del Rey division. Middle of the night. Couple hours of banging, she's done. And, you know, the house is just like all the others so the next morning maybe the shrewder neighbors say, "Hey, Honeybun, was there a house over there yesterday?" "I don't remember, but there's a house there now." "Funny place we live in."

Bohannon's strategy—which, we admit, he hasn't quite yet discussed with Wanda—is to run away with her to this new house. He imagines that the beautiful sameness of their situation will make them invisible to vengeance, which passion—San Lorenzo being a happy place—will eventually pass, and he and Wanda will be able to get on with their life together. No doubt, someday, Roy will even be eager to baby-sit for their children now and then.

"O David, I'm here for you."

So saying, she jumps down and lands in the thickness of Easter lilies and crunchy snails which grow and live at the side of her house. They get in Bohannon's new Buick with the "Greenwood Corporation" emblem on the doors. But before driving to their new home, they stop at the P&X for groceries.

In the produce section they are holding cantaloupes in their hands, judging the fruit of this amazing harvest-land, when they hear a young boy, plainly a child of these suburbs, sing a familiar song in a tender, youthful tenor, "*Mama mia e donnas stranas*" ("My mother is strange women").

> My mother is
> strange women
> I meet in suburban
> supermarkets.
>
> One day she'll
> break down
> before me and
> the staring fruits
> and vegetables,
> and gasp for air,
> sweet air!
>
> Somebody
> Find this woman
> some love!

David and Wanda, heartbroken by this song, are about to put down their melons to applaud his touching performance when up behind them bursts Roy and a mob of neighbors.

"O abandoned creature, you little tramp! You are not worth my grief! But now you'll suffer for playing with me!"

Roy pulls a tire iron out of his pocket because he really is a tough fucker and he knows his rights. But just before he bashes our heroes, some one of the Villagers notices an impropitious banana bulge in Bohannon's trousers. What a time! And then it's just like

109

when I was a kid and the hormones were tearing through my system like low-riders on the strip and erections came unbidden, so I put my hands in my pockets and hoped that none of the guys noticed because if they did, forget it, they'd say, "Look, Curt's got a boner! Curt's got a boner!" And in Bohannon's pathetic situation with Roy already pissed at him things quickly went beyond even that humiliation to "Pants Dave! Let's take a look at it! Big Shot! Tough David D. Bohannon! Pants him everybody!" And they did and everybody stared and laughed at his symptomatic prick leaning out from his belly. Even Wanda, who had been more than once substantially convinced by it, giggled, thus indicating that this was in sooth a very trivial sort of pretending fellow.

Influential friends to the Bohannon family have long condemned this episode as slander or maintained that David's "condition," shall we say, was brought upon him by an experimental antidepressant drug (developed by the same guys who cooked up lysergic acid during the chemical industry's long postwar infatuation with the CIA) for which one of the possible side effects was an ostentatious priapism. We have never strenuously objected to this interpretation of local lore because no one ever suggested that the erection in question was something Bohannon intended. In fact, we have been no more annoyed with the fatuous notion of the East Bay Chapter of the Young Hegelians that the hard-on was an expression of World Spirit. That it was a symbolic, not a clinical erection.

What's crucial to understand is that it was an important and appropriate object for study and that the last thing the Villagers should have done was to ignore it. To turn away. After all, they were San Lorenzo and San Lorenzo was Bohannon and this was therefore Dad's boner winking at them, accessible because of an enormously improbable "revelation."

But turn away is just what they did, laughing, exchanging bawdy quips, Wanda's arm once again in the rightful arm of her husband. In so doing, they turned away from a vision which if properly understood would have been Bohannon's greatest contribution to their welfare and happiness. But it is true that faultless Seeing is rare and difficult to achieve. In fact, it would be another twenty years before the Villagers' children would have a little dope to stimulate even the first possibility of sight.

Are You With Me, Madame Nhu?

She was the sort of woman that fascinated Andy Warhol. Beauty, glamour, wealth, sex, scandal and death. Like golden Marilyn and dead Marilyn. Happy Jackie and tragic Jackie.

Madame Nhu was the notorious and super-seductive sister-in-law to Ngo Dinh Diem, South Vietnamese President during the early days of the American involvement in Vietnam. I was only twelve years old at the time of her greatest notoriety, so my memories of her are hardly archival. I remember that she was seductive and I was seduced. And I remember that when Diem died in the CIA sponsored coup of 1963, she was in Los Angeles after having talked her way across the United States as part of a massive public relations effort. This fact brought out the protective male in prepubescent me. What would she do now? Did she have any money? Was she very sad? Was there anyone to take care of her?

No doubt, *Life* (October 26, 1962) can tell her story better than I.

"Mme. Nhu was born into a staunch and well-placed Buddhist family. Her father, now Vietnam's ambassador to the U.S., was a rich lawyer who saw to it that his daughter (her given name Le Xuan means "Beautiful Spring") lacked for nothing. She was schooled in Europe, principally in France, and even today seems more at home in French than in Vietnamese. All her speeches are written in

112

French. In 1943 she met and married Ngo Dinh Nhu, then head of the Archives and Libraries of Indochina—becoming a Catholic to do so. Nhu is today the all-powerful right hand of his brother, the president.

"Marriage into such an influential family put Mme. Nhu into politics and intrigue up to her pretty neck and she has been in it ever since. In 1946 she was arrested by the Viet-Minh for anti-Communist activities, lived for four months on two bowls of rice a day but later managed to escape."

One of the best anecdotes from this Southeast Asian version of the tale of the poor-little-rich-girl concerns this period of detainment. It seems that the dummy guerrillas under Ho Chi Minh blew up Madame Nhu's piano because they thought it was a radio for communicating with the French. But the godless—and terribly vulgar—Communists played right into her hands, for it was not much later that she would use this incident in her famous "I have a piano" speech.

"Rejoining her husband, she began plotting the return of Ngo Dinh Diem from Europe to Vietnam as chief of government. In July 1954, after the Geneva Conference had split Vietnam into two parts, Diem did come back to take power. He moved into Independence Palace and his brother and Mme. Nhu moved in with him. Because Diem is a bachelor, she was appointed his official first lady.

"Mme. Nhu went briskly and firmly about the business of changing the legal and social status of women in her country. Overwhelmingly Buddhist (about 80%), Vietnam had a solidly patriarchal social structure based on Confucian principles: the husband is good, the wife 'listening.' In practice, this meant that the husband could do almost no wrong, whereas the wife, although '*noi tuong*' ('general of the interior') in her own household, might be repudiated by her husband for a host of reasons including sterility, adultery, lack of respect toward his parents, slander, thievery, jealousy or leprosy. This double standard, as Mme. Nhu put it, made a woman 'an eternal minor, a doll without a soul...a servant without pay.'"

Eventually, Madame Nhu's feminist activism led to the creation of the Vietnamese Women's Solidarity Movement, a group which, in the late days of the Diem regime, had a lot more to do with providing accurate political intelligence than it did with issues of gender justice. This was the period of the "Dragon Lady." She was "molded into her dress like a dagger in its sheath." She referred to the self-immolation of protesting Buddhist monks as "barbecues." She forbade dancing ("Foreigners come here not to dance; dancing with death is sufficient"), yet she wore décolleté form-fitting *ao dais*.

But her most mesmerizing moment followed the arrival of the news about the coup and the assassinations of the brothers Diem and Nhu.

"Was the U.S. behind the coup?" the press asked her.

"I think the devils of hell are against us. If the news is true, if really my family has been treacherously killed with either official or unofficial blessings of the American government, I can predict to you now that the story is only at its beginning. Treason does not pay and nobody can rule Vietnam with just money and puppets."

This prophecy was wasted on the victors of the moment. The radio stations played twist and cha-cha records which oozed out and around the coconut palms lining Saigon's French colonial boulevards. In the bars, the haunts of off duty GIs, girls quickly discarded the plain white smocks that Madame Nhu had required them to wear. They changed back into more alluring, form-clinging dresses so the men could see exactly where a pelvis should be bumped. Outside, a few mangled bodies lay in the gutter.

Do you know the story about the boy who went to market and bought Madame Nhu? It is alleged that in 1965, during the time when Madame Nhu was said to be living in exile outside of Rome, a boy who lived by himself in a large house not far from where you live saw Madame Nhu in a cage at the local market. This particular Madame Nhu was about the size of a large dog. She sat quietly in her cage and chewed on a bone. Next to the cage a merchant was watching the crowd, and the boy asked him if Madame Nhu was for sale.

"Of course," he replied, "Why else am I here? Madame Nhu is excellent, strong and capable of anything. She can build, cook, mend clothes, read you books, teach you French, and what she doesn't know she can learn. And I don't want much for her. $37.95."

The boy didn't haggle and paid in cash. He wanted to take her home at once.

"One moment," the merchant said. "Because you haven't tried to work my price down and rob me of my fair profit, I'm going to tell you something." He leaned close and the boy noticed his breath stank of peanuts. "Look here, you know about Madame Nhu, don't you? You know that she's no good, right?"

"You said she was excellent," the boy said in indignation and confusion.

"Of course, for sure," the merchant said. "Certainly she's excellent. But she is Madame Nhu, after all, and she will always remain Madame Nhu. You have made a shrewd investment, but only if you keep her busy. Every day give her a routine: from this time to that time fix your Cream of Wheat, then play baseball with you, clean your room, make lunch, Three Stooges in the afternoon, pillow fight, dinner, stories, dishes. Something like that every day. If she has time to spare, if she doesn't know what to do, then she is dangerous."

"Oh, I can do that," replied the boy and he took his Madame Nhu home.

Everything went great. Each morning the boy called Madame Nhu who would kneel down obediently. The boy would then dictate a program and she would start the chores right away. She even winked when he opened her dresser and played with her brassieres and lingerie. A boy can't ask for more than that.

Then, after some years, the boy was nearing manhood and he met a friend who suggested they go to the city for fun. In the excitement of the moment, the boy forgot everything. He went to a concert at the Fillmore West featuring Big Brother and the Holding Company and drank Southern Comfort with Janis wailing "ball and chay-yaa-yaa-yain." They ended up sleeping in the park.

The next morning he woke up with a dry eucalyptus leaf clinging to his cheek and promptly puked in the bushes. His friend was gone. He remembered Madame Nhu and rushed home.

As he approached his house, he smelled burning and saw the smoke coming from the kitchen. He ran into the house and saw Madame Nhu sitting on the kitchen floor, her tiny body dirty and naked. She had made an open fire and was roasting the neighbor's child on a spit while basting it in coconut milk and curry.

The boy knew he was really in trouble this time.

Fortunately, the child was known as a troublemaker and general bad kid and he was only a little singed and not completely dead, and even though his parents were mad as heck the boy gave them $25 and everybody else said the kid had it coming. But the boy had had a fright and he was furious with Madame Nhu. His ghastly hangover wasn't helping matters. He ran back home and found her still naked, squatting in the kitchen sink cleaning thick black mud from between her toes. Her legs were cocked awkwardly so that the boy stared directly at the black mat at her groin.

"Where have you been?" she complained. "I didn't know when to go to bed! So, I turned the TV off with a brick. I played your Beatle records with a safety pin. I ate your dog for dinner. I shat on the roof. I took the murdered chickens from the freezer and buried them in the basement, so don't fret about that. But I did inform the police about your other crimes. Your father came over and I gave him a disease. I'm sending pictures and an explanation to your mother, which should arrive shortly after the incubation period. Now, what shall I do today?"

The boy could take no more. He went to the sink and plucked up the filthy Madame Nhu by leg and neck. She screamed and scratched at him but he got her to the front door and threw her down the concrete front steps. Two steps from the bottom, her tiny thin figure came down vertebrae first on the edge of a step and she screamed in ample pain. Howled. Rolled over and over in the middle of the sidewalk. Sort of like those earthworms who make the mistake of crawling onto the concrete during a rainstorm.

The boy of course thought he was done with the naughty Nhu, that he was finally rid of her. But as the afternoon progressed, her wails of anguish continued. He thought she was looking for pity. He'd peek out and see her snaking in a broken way.

Eventually, neighbors and passers-by gathered around this incredible sight: a dirty, naked Asian woman about the size of a large dog, with a broken back, squirming on the sidewalk before his house. A man came up and knocked on his door. He wore overalls and a Cargill seed cap like a Midwesterner. The boy seemed to

117

remember that he had dreamed this all, but it was no dream, it was a story I was told.

"Just what is the idea?" demanded the man. "You can't just leave this little lady out here. I think she needs help. I think her back is broken. People don't ordinarily squirm around like that, like a worm, like a broken snake. Those are strong clues. And if we understood what she said between her cries and groans and sounds like a dog makes, she said that she is owned by you. Well, is she yours? What kind of boy are you, anyway?"

The boy had no idea what kind of boy he was. It had never occurred to him that he might be a kind of boy.

To be sure, the veridical Mme. Nhu did live in seclusion outside Rome (or was it Reno?) and for a short time she was able to charge journalists extortionate sums for a few minutes acquaintance with her shocking wit. Now, as we know, she is outside our purview as if she had never been. Unless, of course, she is still the house guest of Mr. and Mrs. Allen Chase, Hollywood right-wingers, who gave her the run of their pink stucco hillside villa in Bel Air after her husband's sudden death. Sure. Perhaps if we went there and knocked on the door, she'd arrive, perturbed, and say, "I was wondering when someone was going to come. Twenty-six years!"

Are you with us, Madame Nhu? Can you hear me?

Nothing.

And so, you see, there is no grand truth to be taken from the enormous, ephemeral careering of her life, rattling down the corridors of American consciousness. She teaches us what many experiences can and should teach: that knowledge of the good and the true is a matter of rearranging little mortal things. Little mortal things that are as big as things get. For example, as in this case, the consequences of humiliating strangers. Little sexy brown strangers. Even vicious sexy brown strangers of whose conduct we don't approve. Vietnamese. Thais. Libyans. Nicaraguans. I can predict to you now that the story is only at its beginning.

Tales of the Hippies

We stand at the corner of Pasatiempo and Perdido because it marks our present. We're waiting for Now to come along again. You might expect us to stand at the predictable corner of Haight and Ashbury, but that corner marks your victory, a little death and a long fatigue. We'll speak with thirty voices, we'll speak with one voice, we're speechless. You speak for us. After all, you stole our thoughts. Yeah, we recognized you. You're the brain police, aren't you?

Well, go on over to that field, then, the one with the punctures leaking memory, and we'll tell you tales of the hippies.

Becoming Hippy

Clarence! You first. GloBoy we called him in the old days. He used to paint his face. Tell the story about how we got started.

GloBoy unfolds himself and stands. "Well, what started it all was just living in America, the enemy of all dreams." He wore a fez and a jellaba, something tie-dyed, and bell-bottoms. He had rings on his fingers, bells on his toes and a bone in his nose. "I grew up in an East Bay suburb. But it wasn't like the swank suburbs they have in the East, fixed up for the guys who took the train to Madison Avenue in the fifties. This was someplace my father could afford after the war and the merchant marines, while driving a Peter Wheat bread truck for two-fifty an hour.

"I think the thing that saved me and made us, hippies, possible was that very early on I saw that this place had a secret. Maybe a dirty little secret. So, one day I was out riding my bicycle and I stopped before one of the corner street signs. Via Palma and Via Sonya, it read. But what did these words mean? They were telling me something about the place I lived in, I realized, but what? I asked my mom.

"Sonya, I don't understand, dear, but Palma must mean palm so it's Street of Palms.

"Oh, I see. So the trees on that block are palm trees.

"No, no. I think they're sycamores.

"Well, why do they call it Palm then?

"I don't know, for goodness sake! Why is it so important?

"It's a mystery, Mom!

"Oh, she intoned, a mystery, is it? How interesting.

"And why are these names all in Spanish? Don't they want us to know what they mean? And who are they? Mom, who made up these names?

"Then my mother, like many another mother, screamed and washed some dishes.

"But I had to know. I was excited by a curiosity of the intellect for the first time in my life. I went to the library and asked for a Spanish-English dictionary. The old librarian there—a grotesque, knotted, knowing thing—she was suspicious and asked what I could want to know about in Spanish. I was smart enough to see that there was not only a mystery here, but maybe also a conspiracy of these adults. So I lied. I said I had a pen pal in Barcelona. With a frown, she handed over a dictionary, taken from a dark box, but not to be removed from the reference room. I could only browse this strange Spanish-American perplex. They weren't going to allow me to go deep.

"Anyway, my mom was right about the palms. But the word Sonya was stranger. It meant A Street of Dreams. And that was my street! Our little balloon-frame cottage crouched on the Street of Dreams. I was alarmed because all at once I realized I never dreamed, no one ever dreamed on the Street of Dreams. Force of irony!

"That afternoon, when my father crawled from the cab of his Peter Wheat bread van, gray crumbs gripping the rich hair on his forearms, I told him we were being had. We'd been set up for chumps. Like you say, patsies, Dad. The street signs tell me so. He looked at me with his exclusive emotion, exhaustion, then in reply smacked me good and told me to watch TV and shut up.

"The next day I stole that damn dictionary and began my research for real. The things I learned about our town: There was Via Escondido, Street of Secrets or Hidden Things. The meaning there was straight enough. I was really on to something. I had my buddies get on their Stingray bikes and go out all over town making lists and maps of street names. (Even now I can see them peddling off, their hair flowing back, their follicles energized, already a lot like the manes they would soon grow in indignation over this fraud, our lives.) At night, I would decipher what they found with a flashlight, under my bed sheets.

"It was devilish. Via Dolorosa, Street of Sorrowing. Via Descanso, Street of Sleep. Oh, the joke was on us, for sure. Via Bolsa, Street of the Purse. Yes, sad, sleeping shoppers said it all.

"To my surprise, the signs were not limited to one form of truth.

122

The street signs designated fluctuating zones that were coextensive with reality itself. So it wasn't just the grim jokes on our walking middle-class death; there were also signs which appealed straightaway to the possibilities of our changing things, reclaiming life. I explained it all to my buddies one midnight in the garage where we bundled the *Hayward Daily Review* for delivery.

"It's discouraging, I reported to them, the results of my research. They muttered and snapped red rubber bands in their sweaty, ink-stained hands. There is a street here—Teddy, it's on your route—called Via Pecora. That means, Street of the Head of a Sheep. (Teddy got scared and almost cried when he heard that.) What does that mean? Is it some kind of threat? And there's Via Viento, Street of Windy Pride, for our parents.

"Little Stevie raised his hand and asked if there were any streets named for baseball players. Like Via Juan Marichal.

"No, there's no reason for such hope yet, Stevie. Pure play is a long way off for us. Even here, in our meeting place, this garage abuts Via Rincon, or the Street of Lurking, and Via Ventana, the Street of Windows. So, watch it, because they're sure as heck watching us. That's all they need is for us not to take seeing seriously and soon they'll have the only set of eyes in town. However, I can also report with some hope that there is a place called Honda, Street of the Sling for Hurling Stones. We can get started there! And a Via Melena, the Street of Long Hair in Men and Loose Hair in Women. Finally, when our work is done, there is Via Mirabel, Street of Beautiful Sight, a place from which we can see for miles and play our guitars and take consciousness expanding drugs.

"I'd arrived at a rhetorical peak, but my last words confused them. What's he talking about? Conscious-what?

"But just before I lost them, I jumped on a table, on a pile of

123

newspapers, and yelled, Play Ball!

"And with that they all roared, Yayhooh, leaped on their bikes like a dozen Gene Autreys and took off.

"They were long and lonely, those summer months of our rebellion. As Timothy Leary would later command, we'd dropped out. I remember the little camp fires in the cul-de-sac out by the golf course. Our first commune! I remember the bicycles whirring in the dark as boys returned to camp with messages or simply visited from other liberated zones in order to keep spirits high. By then a lot of girls had joined us and—believe it or not—we boys had no objections, we didn't make fun of the way they threw or anything. A change had come over us. They made us feel a lot less alone when the inevitable factors of attrition set in: mothers dragging fellas home by the ear; scary stories circulated by the Dad's Club to undermine our determination, stuff like the Boston Strangler had escaped from jail and announced that now he liked little boys and girls; or, there was a witch doctor uprising in Oakland and the Black God Liborio was coming our way. In my opinion, these were early examples of CIA domestic disinformation. Sad to say, these tactics worked, and by September when it was time to return to school, there were just a few of us left, dirtier and hungrier than Huck Finn ever dreamed of being. Our mothers sat in lawn chairs at our camp periphery, weeping into soggy Kleenexes.

"That was a sight we couldn't take. So we gave up.

"But it wouldn't be long before we'd get back to it, in spite of not wanting to hurt our mothers. This time for keeps. After all, it was only the summer of 1963, and Prince Charming Kennedy was still keeping America amused, the Bay of Pigs was old news, and

Vietnam was limited to the helicopter ferrying operation called 'Waves of Love.' But I remained hopeful. In fact, on the first day of school, I silk-screened a bunch of Oswald Spengler tee-shirts for my pals. We wore 'em expecting the worst, but the teachers didn't get it! Didn't even bat an eye! It was then I knew for sure that it was possible to be subtle enough to be free, to discover a line of flight and use it. Soon, we did."

Becoming Becoming

Wild. That's how it was all right. Now, Dandelion, what about our glory? What about the summer of love before the Summer of Love? How about life before the portable cam crews caught it, refracted it once or twice, and left this twist of image that became a virus indistinguishable from the national infection?

"Oh, you mean before the arrival of the creeps who loved us to death?"

That's right.

"Dig it. Well, GloBoy had our beginnings about right. We began in doubt. Hey, mom and dad, we said, you tryin' to say this place is reality? Far out. What a joke. Nice trick to play on your own kids.

"But what GloBoy was talking about was a political doubt. There was another kind of doubt as well, stimulated by our first teeny tokes on the weed, man, pot. Don't get me wrong, dope can't take you where you need to go, but it sure is a start, a little jump start, something to break through the crust. We'd look at our shoes and say, What's shoes? Everything looked strange and new, as if seen for the first time. Everything posed the same question: What is it to Is? What's 'izzzing'? What is clothes? What's Cheez Whiz? What's high school? What's 'prompt free delivery'? We'd get stoned and think of something like—garden hose—and then we'd laugh like crazy because something so silly existed and people paid money for it. Hoo hee!

"Deeper, profounder curiosities came to our attention as well. Little complexities of unreason which argued that the way we'd understood the world to that point was false. Once we were sitting around watching 'The Munsters' on a collapsing Sylvania console with the sound off and the Mothers of Invention on the stereo, when out of nowhere it occurred to me that 'pain' doesn't make sense. That's a fact. It's not logical. Who would have guessed? I mean, we're used to thinking that there is a basic logic to pain because it tells us not to do something, right? It's the body's way of saying, 'Hey, you're messing up! You're violating the integrity of the flesh envelope.'

"Then I thought, fine, but why does that logic require excruciating pain? Like say if you accidentally cut off your hand with a saw, you don't need agony to know you made a serious mistake. So, pain I understand, but that pain we call agony seems beyond what is required. How dumb does the body think we are, anyway?

"Finally, at the profoundest level, drugs stimulated the insights that caused doubt about everything. Great Doubt. There were times when nothing made sense. All is loneliness, as Moondog used to say. It was a loneliness that was not just feeling alone, but like not understanding what was happening at all. While this was scary, it wasn't all bad, because it pushed us not to suicide, but to getting it together and figuring out a response to the Great Nothing, something beyond taking the credit card for a shopping spree.

"That's right, you got it: we 'experimented' with 'alternative life-styles' in 'hippie pads' and 'communes.' We called it living together.

126

"By the way, did you know that in these the quiet days of Reagan Good Feelings, so far beyond the time of the rattling hippies, in dismay over the lack of protest from the living, the dead themselves have begun to complain? Authorities aren't eager for it to be known, but in many municipal graveyards graffiti has begun to appear mysteriously, the same message over and over, a resentful expression of disappointment from the moribund: LIFE DOES NOT LIVE.

"There are other signs. Every once in a while, an article will crop up in the newspaper. Subtle stuff like attendants at animal hospitals have begun to notice that the dead animals are shrieking in outrage while they are being fired in the incinerators. One veterinarian even confessed, 'I have often heard a scream or meow from cats when they were accidentally dropped even though I knew for a fact they were dead.' Oh, some scientists have tried to explain that this is just the expulsion of air from the animal's lungs. But don't you believe it. The animals are pissed. We could learn a thing or two from their rage.

"This isn't what you asked me to talk about, is it? I'm wandering. But wandering is so beautiful! In fact, maybe wandering is what was at the heart of our movement. My thesis is in my digression. Yeah, I like that. That's hip. It would be a betrayal of the story of our best times to tell it as a 'straight' story anyway. So I'll tell it as one long digression. There's the infinite in that. Here goes:

"Well, the way we heard it from Ecstatic Tom who stood at the corner of 11th Street and Avenue A who heard it in Katmandu and elsewhere is that Kerouac and American Zen died so that Big Al and Carol Doda could sin 'tits, booze, smack and professional pussy' which was real depressing for awhile but Spirit is resourceful and knows how to stay cool till the time is well furnished and the rent's paid in advance then it beckoned new age mutants forth from

127

simmering dumplings in the Panhandle or they flew in on UFOs and founded a tax exempt non-profit religious foundation under California state law for the ecstatic transformation of earth into paradise love gifts planted the paradisal sanctuaries for all wild-flower people forever they called it Electric Tibet or a 'trippy body cream for groovy loving' depending on my mood some park benches grew pranksters who fed our heads and introduced you to the only god in the world for you she was special you were shy and said 'pleased to meet you' anyhow behind the sheer Indian print sheet a pot was boiling Digger stew for dinner they served a bowl and the little alphabet pastas spelled out Free Frame of Reference solid! but sometimes admit it you'd start talking and regretting what you said and feelings would pile up at your side like dead birds and I'd talk and regret what I said and we'd go back and try to correct it to infinity total feedback that for instance wasn't hip that wasn't cool that wasn't far out or out of sight that wasn't groovy that was sadness but when you said take the methedrine hence that's foe to man that solved the problem and besides she always forgave and he gave us a hug so twelve of us turned out the lights and threw the Indian print on top and we wriggled out of our jeans and the pot bubbled in plain view although no one was looking at it we grabbed a body and if it had a foot we said I like feet and if it had a bicameral mind we said I like bicameral minds and if it was the Father of History we said I like the Father of History finally you got your body confused with mine like putting on the wrong hat they said I looked silliest of course I felt awkward I had no idea how to enjoy your herbal tea then someone said 'We plain Americans' and made us laugh 'this great land of ours' 'you beardnik' hee hee hee we were some real odd numbers no doubt we laughed and groped till the surface of the sheet looked just like the boiling of the pot beside it both kept us warm now that was Happy.

"That was happy, okay. But you all know well what happened next. Someone turned the light on. 'Hey, who turned the light on? I can't see a thing!' That was our last joke. We all sat up like twelve lucid sleepers to a nightmare and looked to our right as if the meaning of our dream were written on the wall. And there at the door stood an oily messiah, his hand still on the light switch as if it were our collective heart, an omnivorous gleam in his eyes, like a coyote thinking 'Bunnies!'

"Then he said, 'Hi there. My name's Charlie.'"

Death of Hippy

And last there is our sad boy, Groovy, to tell of our end. Groovy stands, and his head is mutilated, stove in by a brick. It happened while he slept on the sidewalk before the Blue Unicorn, the very place of the first hippy sighting. Too much electric tea. He passed out. Then he became a mortar to someone's pestle.

"I'm sorry. I know I don't look too good."

A bit of brain protruded, and an eye dangled from a gristle of nerve.

"This is what guys like Charlie brought us to. Even me, the Lysergic Lenin, the Leader of the Laughers, not even I was pure enough to survive. I heard it was my own shadow, gone confused, that rose in the flame of the street lamp, took a brick and played me primitive. Is that true?

"Living in America. It's like having a little brother who's twice your size and moronic to boot. He follows you around like that Lenny character and every time you discover some new way to be, he apes it. If we could only stay one change ahead! Maybe then the goon USA would get confused and bored and leave us alone. Then, if there were enough of us blooming quietly for long enough, seed to the wind, we could lift up one day when we were just too much, solid gone, too wild and original to be denied, and say, 'Surprise! Remember us?'

"Well, we tried to be the ones who could jump over their own shadows, we tried to be flower powered Jack-be-Nimbles, but we ended up more ineptly earthbound than we liked. We got old quick and slow on the up beat, syncopated in a way that was indistinguishable from clumsy. Then we were easy prey for the Company. Listen to my case.

"When I felt the heat in '67, when I sensed the warp setting in, a mutation fathered by old Walter Cronkite, I split for South America to save my own skin, or split maybe to save a sliver of the genetic code that might one day, after our public demise, be used to get the whole thing started again. Yeah, I imagined it might one day come down to a contest between my genes and Walt Disney's cryogenic DNA. Unca Walt lives!

"Anyhow, I split for the South American principality of Panamania, there to lay low until the hour was ripe. But the Man is wise. He's making a list and checking it twice. He knew I'd head for Panamania before I did. He picked me up at the airport in a taxi. I should have known when I saw the silver box on the dashboard, right next to the outrageous meter, in which he was to bring back locks of my offending hair to Mr. Hoover.

"What I didn't figure about South America was that it could be hotter than the heat I fled. Everything in the little village I stayed in—walls, bridges, trees—seemed just a degree from decomposing, melting away. For comfort, I stayed crouched in the corner of a grimy cantina, trying to cool myself by drinking warm mescal and pressing my face against an infectious adobe wall. Occasionally, I'd sleep briefly, and once I woke to find a swollen, malignant tendril from some voracious jungle vine gripping my wrist powerfully.

"One day as I sat in that cantina, reading William Burroughs and sipping gin, a man—the Man, I thought—came in and perched on the tall, spare stool across from me. Overhead, a fan labored to mix the thick Panamanian air. I couldn't see his face, for he wore one of those plaited hats made of the young leaves of the jipijapa which natives hawked on the street for a few centavos or a fruit that hadn't yet rotted.

"I tried to pull myself back into the gloom of my corner. I was frightened. I knew what came next. His hand would slip inside his coat and produce a pistol with which I would be executed. This was something I wished to avoid. Slowly, I began inching my hand through the darkness of my body to my own revolver (guns are sold in great piles, like carts of plantains, in Panamanian markets and I'd bought one).

"Then, just as my own hand found the humid butt of my gun, his right hand moved casually beneath his jacket. I sprang forward, urging my gun before me, gripping it vulgarly, demanding from it a single dull explosion, rather like the sound of a melon splatting on pavement.

"One shot was all I needed. It struck him square in the face. He toppled off his perch and landed on his right shoulder, flinging his right arm to his side. I went immediately to see who it was I'd killed. In his hand where I thought I'd find his weapon, I found only a tiny black pear—round, perfectly ripe—of the sort which were frequently used as currency in that cantina. He was about to buy something from me. He wasn't going to shoot me at all. He wanted a glass of the viscid, tropical gin I drank. I looked for his wound.

"There I found something fantastic. Instead of the dingy, redundant bullet hole I expected, I saw that at the point of entrance, square in the middle of his face, his flesh had—what other word is there for it?—blossomed! There in the middle of his face a flower of meat had exuberantly bloomed with fervid petals as red as prime beef. When I looked closer, I saw that the petals themselves, which arched elegantly from the center like a languid anemone or a violent sunflower, were themselves a complexity of really beautiful cells as one finds in the voluptuous oranges of eastern China, only here they were of the crimson color and the gelatinous, pulpy quality of a pomegranate. Yes, indeed, a pomegranate of meat.

"But this was but one of the wonders this man had in store for me. Beneath his coat, projecting from his body as if from a dead log of wood, was a finely layered, opulently colored vest of the silky and almost translucent fruit-bodies, the beautiful white anastomosing sporophores, the blood-red fructifications, the edible glutinous cuticles, the greenish gills, the fine radial striations, hymenial surfaces and thin-walled hyphae of macrofungi, of mushrooms.

"The next thing, I was in a hospital, because a bullet had grazed my own temple. The gentle, concerned doctors of Panamania explained—when I asked what I could possibly be doing there— that I'd shot myself, attempted suicide. Of the other fellow they knew nothing. They also suggested that I should stop eating the tiny, pulsing, radiogenic worms which slept in the deeps of my mescal bottles.

"Bummer. Desperate, desperate, double bummer.

"So I went back to the States, back to the Haight. It wasn't long before I died for good. Head stove in with a brick. Strange. But the one thing I'm not sure of is, did I do it to myself again? Do you know, mister? Do any of you understand?"

Easy, Groovy. You're okay, man. We're with you. We love you. We all drew around him and gave him a dozen hugs. Are you happy, pal, Mr. Brain Agent? Look how upset he is. Finally, though, Groovy pushed us aside to say one last thing.

"I knew this chick who used to smoke a lot. She got sick once and had to have a serious operation, but her lungs were so bad from the smoking that she couldn't pass the balloon test for the anaesthesia. So she risked not surviving the operation.

"Her doctor considered the situation and said, 'If you don't have the operation, you'll die. So, we'll operate, and if you die because you've wasted your health on cigarettes, well, fuck you.'

"I would like to say something similar to the species. Humans, I mean. We hippies failed, maybe, but we tried something amazing that was, even if just for a little minute, noble and alive. But if the rest of you have ignored all the death in our culture—mental death, physical, economic, environmental, military, judicial, spiritual— and if you've concerned yourself only with getting high, getting laid, and making money to buy shit, if you've found no way large or small to make even a little revolution, a tiny mutation, a single rip in the membrane of our shared sausage casing, then fuck you."

In Thailand: an Autobiographical Statement

I was welcomed to Thailand by Coca-Cola: An enormous billboard featuring Thailand's most popular rock band relaxing with cans of Coke. Later, at the Impala Hotel in Bangkok, I was given a more authentic Thai greeting by mosquitoes. I found one or two, but others were small, silent and smart enough to elude and survive. Silent, that is, until I turned the lights out, at which point they buzzed in with all of the subtlety displayed by Japanese business-men reaping Thai baht over coffee and cigarettes. When I awoke the next morning, there was a set of bites in the shape of a lotus leaf on my pale chest. The bites looked like the perforations on a customs document.

That afternoon, I was the only hotel guest at the swimming pool reading Hegel's *Lectures on the Philosophy of Religion*. (Sidney Sheldon has been translated into Thai.) At night, Western tourists go to Patpong to watch teenage Thai girls do things with their cunts that I can't do with my hands. (Cf. *Swimming to Cambodia*, Spalding Gray.) I wanted to go, too! My fellows, you palefaces, what's my name? Why can't we speak to one another? Take me along!

To console myself, I had a beer, tangy shrimp and little red clams that were precisely vaginas, then returned to my room to watch the national news. I couldn't understand the announcer, so I could only wonder why, for example, Danny Ortega appeared tired and sad. He'll look like Reagan by the end of the decade. (How was it that he emerged from the years of fighting Somoza looking like a sixteen-year-old?) I opened Hegel again and a large fly buzzed from between the pages. I took it as a good omen and felt suddenly glad that I hadn't made the nightclub scene. I was going to find something in that book, by god. I'd find and kill the fly later.

Really, folks, as I'm sure you sensed, this claim of "sudden gladness" is paltry bravado. I felt very lonely in my VIP hotel suite with four double beds and two TVs neither of which could talk to me, both of which reminded me that I was in Thailand. On some nights I was so intimidated by the plurality of beds that I couldn't even sleep in one. After all, what might the maid deduce from my choice? Sometimes pubic hairs curl like script on bed linen. You know that. You've seen it and been stunned by the implications. I couldn't face the sneaky connotations possible in Thai script, rooted in Pali and notorious Sanskrit. So, I didn't dare to turn back the beautiful sheets. I tried to sleep lightly so that I didn't dent the pillow. On one night I was so successful that I lost myself. "Curtis!" I called. "Yes!" "Curtis!" "Yes!"

Let me tell you a story. It didn't happen to me while I was in Thailand, but never mind that. I was down in Songkhla staying in a 100-baht room at the Holland Bar. Fat Dutch guy owned the place. He catered to an upscale gay clientele and their native boys. He owned a VCR and nice color TV but only one tape, a Madonna concert tape live in Italy. (Prime Minister Chatichai ousted ex-Prime Minister Prem on the strength of his commitment to "Material Girl" as the new Thai national anthem.) For my part, I grew to know the muscles in Madonna's arms. By the end of my stay, I was convinced she had fallen for me. I think we could have worked something out, but I was damned busy with the boys. I was straight as a string till I found myself in Thailand. It started out with suck jobs with fellows on the beach. It was all good fun for the boys, although none forgot the service charge. By the end of my stay, I was balling four boys per day, none of them a bit better than they needed to be. It only took two weeks for my disease to depopulate most of southern Thailand even to the Burma mountains that look like angular camels. Only a few women remained in scattered, stubborn rural pockets, places where JELL-O still causes a stir. I was asked to leave and agreed it was probably best for all concerned. New boys are being smuggled back into southern Thailand in the flat woven baskets traditionally used for growing silkworms. Damndest thing, the boys take on some of the worm's identity in the process. Little brown froggy native boys, like Joyce said, wriggling over each other and lifting themselves to be fed. When I learned of this strategy, my fatigue and distress became extreme because I knew it would all just have to be done again. That's the misery of mastery here in post-imperial, new colonial Thailand, where the tourist is sahib.

I am tired. I think of being in Thailand and my eyes get heavy. I sleep. On the morning of my second day in Thailand I wake feeling special. I go downstairs for breakfast with the *Bangkok Post* and read that the Panchen Lama has died. The search for his reincarnate successor has begun. For a moment, I feel quite pleased with myself.

The official purpose of my visit to Thailand was to lecture at campuses of Srinakarinwirot University on modern American literature. They wanted to know about the short story. When they said the words "short story," I almost believed that such a thing existed. They're so innocent. They wept when I told them that American literature was dead. No time lost grieving in America, I'll tell you. The undergraduate students wear uniforms here, the girls white blouses and blue skirts. I was lecturing one day on postmodernism and the critique of the structure of reference in Saussure when I realized that they weren't understanding a word I said. I informed them that in fact I was speaking in tongues, glossolalia. We were having a religious experience. Oh! They were pleased. So that's what this was! A light blue sexual pall descended upon us. We were in love. I fell upon a young girl whose brown legs I'd been admiring. To my surprise, she was wearing edible panties. Prawn flavored. I took my first nibble and the class began to giggle. I asked if I was doing something wrong. Apparently, in Thailand the head of the professor should never be below the heads of the students. I'd made quite a mistake. But they forgave me because I was a farang (foreigner) and was expected to make humiliating errors of custom. Needless to say, I immediately returned to my august position at the front of the class, heads above the throng, and continued with my probings at enlightenment.

After the lecture, I was taken to lunch by my Thai colleagues, at which meal devastating evidence was presented that I was not human, thus placing the status of my grant in grave question. The wife of one of the Foreign Affairs administrators asked me if I liked Thailand.

"Yes, of course, very much."

"And what do you like most?"

"The food is wonderful. I like the spices."

"And have you tried a Thai girl yet?"

Were Thai girls like potato chips? "No I haven't. I'm afraid that if I have one, I'll need to have another. Next thing you know, the bag will be empty."

"Bag?" she inquired.

I smiled enigmatically, trying to out inscrutable her.

My hosts talked among themselves until they reached a conclusion.

"What are you all talking about?" I asked.

"My wife says you are not human."

"Not human?"

"Yes, yes! Not human! Our friends agree."

I didn't know their friends. One was an accountant for a Thai-Texas oil concern. He'd been to Dallas. That seemed to make him objective. That seemed to make his opinion count for a lot.

"Tell her that I am human. Still human. Human anyway. I am human in spite of the facts."

He thought about it and then declared, "This can not be said in Thai."

I wanted to argue that it sure as bloody hell could (I'd read it in the Abhidharma, their own sacred commentary on the teachings of Lord Buddha), but I didn't want to start a row. So I conceded that it was possible that I was not human. I was mortified. If I had confessed to my mortification, perhaps they would have agreed that I was a dead human at least.

Speaking of dead people, I had dinner at the Oriental Hotel, below its famed Joseph Conrad suite, with a Fulbright scholar about to return to the States. Actually, to Knoxville, Tennessee. He told me that he had written an essay for delivery to the Rotary Club called "Thailand: Land of Contrasts."

His little title infuriated me. "Don't be stupid," I scolded. "Say what you mean. Thailand is not a land of contrasts, it is a land of contradictions. There's a difference, you know."

He didn't care for my tone and before you knew it (certainly before I knew it) we were in one hell of an argument over whether or not Orlando, Florida, was vulgar. I don't believe in vulgarity, but I was more than happy to take up its cause if that meant that I could attack Disney World. We parted feeling like father and son.

I was in Mahasarakram, near Laos, one early morning eating my usual artery choking "American breakfast" of fried eggs and hot dogs when I saw for the first time the daily procession of monks in single file, saffron robes blazing gloriously, making their way with their bowls past the rows of open-air restaurants where they collect their meals. They do so quietly. The shopkeepers appear excited and happy to be able to give the food. There is no sense of loss. They don't anguish over the grains of rice they will have to pinch from subsequent paying customers in order to balance the ledger. Somehow, the understanding survives that to give to the monks is miraculously TO GIVE TO THEMSELVES.

Mahasarakram is far enough out of the tourist circuit that I was about the only Westerner in town. It did not feel threatening but oddly exciting to be the only white among so many Asians. I felt almost a sense of relief. I felt for no good reason that they were responsible for me. It was their job to see that I met no harm. I also felt this ridiculous urge to talk to them all about the CIA, just to let them know that not all Americans approved of its sinister international bungling. (Maybe no Americans approve. Maybe that's why there is a CIA. A government off the shelf, as they say. Bobbing in the Chesapeake.) Well, after all, it was my first opportunity to speak to the world. I shouldn't be judged too harshly if I acted like hostages do when they get out and say, "Forget that videotaped confession. They made me say it. Here's what I really think."

I think that if I had seen one of the beautiful orchid monks, full of his monkish understanding and his concern for the people, explaining to the shopkeepers—in exchange for his rations—that this is exploitation, and this is ideology, and this is the Repressive State Apparatus, I would have felt better. And as for revolutionary struggle, what do you imagine wrathful deities are all about? Oh, and can you imagine when those 500,000 juvenile prostitutes decide to drive out the foreign devils? A streetwise, street-tough children's crusade. Boxer Rebellion II.

One night, back in Bangkok, I was offered one of Thailand's contradictions for dinner. We guests were offered "Chicken Lolita." What should I have made of this delicacy? It made me think as much of Jonathan Swift's "Modest Proposal" as of Nabokov's kindly classic about "nymphets." Then I thought of Greek myth in which revenge is acquired by serving your child to you, her head under a platter, her thin lips buzzing their last childish tune. I chose the vegetarian fried rice, drank a weak cup of tepid Chinese tea, left a generous tip, and crept back to my room feeling that I had been damned lucky that time.

One last story in Thailand. Night before I left. Cruising Patpong with boys and girls rippling behind me, clutching to my arms like holiday streamers. A largish crowd ahead, being offered something for sale. But too excited. It's a squarish woman with a shoe box the contents of which is for sale for 2,000 baht. It's a kitty. 2,000 baht for a kitty? No, it's a tiger cub, and not more than a week or two old. Was it stolen from its den? Was the mother killed? Was this woman right to speculate that she could sell it to the gathered farang?

I returned to my hotel to pack for the long return trip to Normal, Illinois, flying back across the international date line into last night. I rubbed some aloe vera into the still sanguine lotus leaf of mosquito bites. Thailand had left its mark on me. I determined that when I was asked, "How was Thailand?" I would answer by lifting my shirt to show the inflamed scar leeching to my translucent breast like a bloodsucking annelid worm. (Of course, my friends would take it for a hickey from some nipple sucking Ganymede. Because I'm not human, I'm doomed to be misunderstood.) My fear was that even though I had resisted the urge to smuggle out one of Thailand's treasures—ivory, sapphires, exotic birds, opium, antiquities, a Buddha image, a tiger, a fifteen-year-old girl—I sported this bloody badge which might attract the suspicion of a customs agent, who might conclude that it was the mark of a criminal understanding. I was damned sure leaving with something questionable. It would even seem just to me if it were claimed that this was a form of espionage. I admit that I had knowledge of the appropriate export documents available at the Ministry of Foreign Affairs, but I'd piddled away my time and now I'd just have to risk it. Wish me luck.

Four Theses on the Fate of the Sixties

"Not unlike the Californians who build houses on top
of the San Andreas fault, they await disaster."

—Landon Jones, *Great Expectations*

Thesis one

Because irony knows no limits and recognizes an easy mark when
it sees one, it is certain that the sixties generation—raised on
revolution and yearning in the enervated eighties for its return—
will find, when revolution does return, that they are the ones to be
overthrown.

That's about the size of it. If the Pentagon were to be levitated
now, like Allen Ginsberg, Abbie Hoffman and the Fugs did in
1967, when it reached shoulder level out scampering like shame-
faced mice and roaches would come guys and gals who used to wear
their hair, their "freak flags," down to their butts. Which isn't to

imply that any of the brothers and sisters actually work in the Pentagon now. It's still a closed club, and our photographs—sticking a flower in the barrel of a National Guard rifle, or blowing a "J" for the benefit of nerdy FBI photographers—are still, even at this late date, all too vividly of us. But you don't have to live in the "belly of the beast" to benefit from the beast's reign. Now, there you've got us.

My own story is as good an illustration as any. I started out in mass communications, B.A. from Iowa State, then moved to the West Coast along with everybody else twixt eight and twenty-eight from Grand Rapids and Bismarck and Boise and Topeka, for god's sake, with just a fragment of the freak infection. And why not? They were discovering new sexes in San Francisco. Who wouldn't want to be in on that? Like, say, Number 17: Bike-dyke: Harley to the waist, femniverous fem on up. When a straight would say the phrase "opposite sex," we'd laugh and laugh. We were more interested in the "apposite sex." Which one from the gallery is to your taste, monsieur? You'll take them all! *C'est très bon!* Monsieur has the Body Eclectic!

What's more, they were creating one-a-day multiple manifestoes to defend their new and improved freedoms. It wasn't all mute, inglorious praxis. The new philosophy got to me in Ames in a Moby Grape song called "Naked If I Want To." Some Revolutionary Youth agents smuggled it through the State Police blockade at the edge of town, out by Sambos, in a Frank and Nancy Sinatra album jacket. I must have listened to that song a hundred times in my bedroom, with the headphones on and the door locked and mom removed, curly characters of marijuana trekking up and down the narrow nerve ledges leading to my cerebral cortex. Finally, I heard the message meant just for me in the groove between cuts three and four on side one. My personal instructions detailing the role I was to play in the Revolution.

I've never been more dangerous before or since. I moved to California and used my mass media preparation to get a job with a Romper Room syndication up in Sonoma. I was Miss Alice. At night, I lived in a big commune in Cazadero, but by day it was strictly Miss Alice, replete with magic mirror and Misters Do and Don't Bee. Buzz, buzz, buzz, brother.

You know, Romper Room for Christ's sake. The kid's show. Jesus, time is sinister.

But producer Bert Claster and company didn't give a shit what I was really like or what I did in my off-hours, as long as I moved the Romper Room Official Highly Educational Toy line:

"Jimmy, if you had a magic mirror like Miss Alice's, what would you like to see?"

"I'd like to see a war."

"Do you mean really be there?"

"Yes, but if they asked, I'd say I was a sightseer."

"That's nice, Jimmy. You know, one of the things you'd see if you went to war is napalm. Napalm is like jell-o made out of fire. Don't touch napalm, boys and girls. And do you know what napalm is made of? Gasoline! Just like the gasoline daddy puts in your car. So, if you can't go to war, at least you can play with this Romper Room miniaturized gas station made by our friends at Hasbro!"

"Stick it, Miss Alice. I want an assault rifle."

I thought this kind of program was in its own way subversive. Kids aren't dumb. They catch on. But some people don't have a sense of humor. The liberal lackeys from Action for Children's Television (ACT) claimed it was wrong for us to use the teacher as a commercial announcer and wrong for the child participants to demonstrate the products. Well, of course it was wrong. But in my hands—this is what those do-gooders couldn't see—such a show was a radioactive pea meant to simmer under consumer culture's cushioned fanny till one day, whoops, a little malignant tidbit would leap up and goose them.

Anyway, the ACT protests to the National Association of Broadcasters worked. We tried a number of things to save the show. I suggested we use midget cyborgs instead of children. Who cares if a cyborg eats sugary breakfast food or plays with a simulated howitzer at recess? Unfortunately, I overestimated the enemy. The dumb-fucks didn't even notice. Half the time the borg's little smiles were so crooked they nearly fell off their faces. Their smiles were like nameplates held by a screw on one side only, swinging stiffly from a cheek. Some of the cyber-boys-and-girls even seemed to acquire parents mysteriously who came full of duty to pick up their dense darlings at the studio gate. At any rate, my gambit failed, I was fired, the studio was folded up and carted away and who the hell knows what happened to the toddling droids. Probably got MBAs at Berkeley. Probably VPs with GMC and Citicorp by now. They must have been lonely at first, but from what I can see they're doing a fine job of reproducing their kind.

Needless to say, being fired from Romper Room didn't leave me with nothing to do. For awhile I tried less covert, more overt means of subverting. I joined the Student Mobilization Committee and the Students for a Democratic Society and the Yippies and RYM and the Peace and Freedom Party and I even belonged to an "affinity" cadre of the Weatherman (about which more later). Nonetheless, by 1973 or so all these revolutionary fronts seemed insubstantial. We shot our wad on Chicago and the Cambodian

145

incursion and thereafter it was all postcoital *tristesse*. We were once again rattling around in the hollowness of the American century. I guess we learned that being a World Historical Individual is a tricky career option. It's tough intending a revolution. You feel pretty silly when it appears that after a decade of struggle instead of Fidel's severe play all you've got to show is a sappy Happening complete with beads, buzz and your own hip paparazzi in paisley. So, starting around 1974, we the disappointed started getting jobs. Countercultural as all get out at first, to be sure. But eventually it was hard not to see that what we'd also almost inadvertently acquired in the universities—organizational skills, knowledge and a capacity for insight—the auto-, techno- and bureau-crats were willing to pay really a lot of money for.

The rest is well known. Our deviant brilliance was given over to High Tech, Apple, Information Industry scams with wild names like Pacific Telesis, precocious Mozarts of the Wall Street money pits, Cuisinart, BMW, and laser disc players for our reissued copies of *Sgt. Pepper* and *Surrealistic Pillow*. Meanwhile, like a bunch of grannies, we have packed away in a little dusty chest, up in the attic, mementoes that we will one day find with moist eyes: a yellowing photo of a certain boy with a ponytail and a mouse-eaten copy of *Chairman Mao's Red Book*.

So, what am I saying? If what we wanted was power, son of a gun, we got it after all. We're the new educated aristocracy and we will be for some time to come. Ronald Reagan is finally gone, therefore World War II is at last over. We rule the roost. We possess all the shibboleths of power and privilege. Which wouldn't be so bad (maybe we earned it), except that I keep hearing something. Don't you hear something? A kind of scratching? I hope it's not those little brown people again. The other day I was leaving late and there were hundreds of them outside in the twilight. Security was having a hell of a time. They had copies of *The National Enquirer* in their hands. They had Elvis t-shirts. They wanted to talk about the return of basic American values in Spanish and Vietnamese. They were roaring Van Halen on ghetto blasters made in Korea. They had discount coupons for Ponderosa Steak House sticking out of their pockets. They wanted more MEAT. I think I saw Pat Robertson behind them, and he thought this was really funny. But more than anything else, they wanted IN.

I turned to Mr. Jackson, our Director of Security, and placed my hand on his sweat drenched shoulder. You should have seen the stress on the poor guy's face. I said to him, "You know, Jackson, we need to talk to the Vice President about a raise for you. This is some job you've got."

Thesis two

When the parents of the sixties generation die, their aging children will experience a delayed authenticity crisis. For years they have defined themselves against the values of their parents. Now when they push there will be nothing to push against.

As for my relationship with my father, believe me, Sylvia Plath had it good. My dad actually worked in munitions development for Westinghouse. Imagine. A perfectly useful degree in engineering and the best thing he could think to do with it was design "ordnance," as they called it. New and improved delivery systems for cluster bombs, smart bombs, needle bombs, heat-seeking missiles, defoliants, chemicals and all of the other clever devices of "conventional" warfare.

It was like having Thor for a father. Mr. Thunderbolt. Mr. Big Bertha. Mr. Surface-to-Air Missile for his high-flying daughter. It wasn't until I discovered Weatherman in '69 that I evened the odds. Wargasm in the streets!

You probably won't believe me when I tell you, but my father was delighted when he learned that I'd joined Weatherman. It was like he thought, "Oh boy, no punches held now."

By 1970, I was totally underground. I was living in Tucson, teaching at night, plotting attacks on the Man during the day and using whatever time remained to put together my next identity and scout out my next location (Pittsburgh and the Women's Militia, I believe). Well, somehow Da got a message through. I was to go to a bank in Tempe and use a key he'd sent me to open a security box. Gee, I thought, maybe the old guy's going to help me out after all. A little cash for his daughter on the lam. Amazing as it sounds, he booby-trapped the safe deposit box. Out came a noxious gas and an indelible ink marking both me and the poor bank clerk who was helping me. Inside was a note reading "Arrest this lesbian bitch commie." I ate the note, helped the clerk from the vault, and was lucky enough to slip away in the chaos.

So then it was my turn. I persuaded an IRA comrade (in the states shopping for guns) to help me with Jerry Rubin's command to "kill your parents." We conceived a greeting for Da and sent it where he lived, up in plush Lake Forest (the ritzy suburb north of Chicago owned by the dead animal magnates Swift and Armour). He fed plastic explosives with a tiny detonator to my dad's favorite bulldog, then sent him scampering back into the house. A pretty mess, I understand.

Over the next year and a half we exchanged all sorts of witty destruction. In some ways, I felt closer to him during that period than I ever had before. But this was obviously an untenable closeness, an intolerable mutuality, for which I paid with two fingers lost to a diabolical grenade. So, I had no choice but to get serious, look for closure. "That's it, Da," I said. "I'm going to kill you."

I started by buying a pair of wing tips from Florsheims. I packed them like a cannon muzzle with anything that had the right sort of bite. I personally filed twenty ignition keys to Fleetwood Cadillacs until you could open a can of tuna with them. That was shrapnel, that was the silver bullet for this ghoul. Then the grey explosives, tender as Playdoh.

I was just walking out of my room, holding the wing tips gingerly, like I was bringing out father's slippers, when I saw one of my militant sisters, in distress, holding a message in her hands.

"I'm sorry, hon," she said, "but it says here that you're father has died. Aneurysm in the brain. Here's the obit."

When I reached for it, I must have been in shock, because I dropped the kiloton footwear. The only reason we didn't go, then and there, in a horrendous blast, is that the shoes fell into a crevice, an abyss. I looked down and I could see them, two fatal, comical, brown wing tips. Falling and falling.

Thesis three

Demographics indicate that the generation that prided itself for being anti-institution and especially anti-family, will—because the Baby Boom sired only a Baby Bust; because it concerned itself only with the growth of Self; and because it did only "its own thing"—

149

that this generation will in its old age find itself with no one to care for it. It will find itself finally dependent precisely on institutions.

Even now suburban development soothsayers, sages of real estate speculation, are planning elaborate nursing colonies that make the old suburbs look like the most original and extreme outskirts of the Imagination. These old folks homes of the future will be made only of plastic. (That's salt in the wound.) Whole houses will emerge from a single mold, furniture included. Takes five minutes. They set up the wax casting and pour in this purple liquid from a huge dumpster, just like the elephants we used to get from the machines at the zoo. Only you can't move that chair, you can't rearrange the living room, and the pillows are a plasticine nightmare, hard as your arteries. The TV is permanently "on," reruns of "Happy Days," except it's about the eighties and stars the son of Michael J. Fox and the great-grand-daughter of Barbara Eden. And when you protest, "What about Jimi and Janice?" the Big Nurse laughs and searches for hallucinogens—"You're not sneaking mushrooms again, are you? Naughty, naughty." Yes, it is Nurse Ratched. It is she who will have the last laugh.

Thesis four

For the generation of the sixties, to be old may someday have all the possibilities of youth.

Look here. Consider this For Your Eyes Only. It's a secret the future will confess.

Listen. The nursing colonies were bad news. "God," we groaned. "It's Kafka." This was amusing and ironic as all get out. The institutionalizing of the anti-institutional. But even though irony knows no limits, it knows no allegiances either. So, let's talk last laughs. Let's see if this dialectic has really flipped its last flop.

I and many unrelated others were taken to the Huey P. Newton Nursing Colony in Elko, Nevada, shanghaied in a Snacks for Seniors van. Elko is a desolate place composed of a redundancy of free-floating brush and everything gray, as if a kindergartner being taught colors had been instructed to "put all the gray pieces in Nevada." There was one sidewalk leading out of the Colony over to the Strawberry Fields Shopping Mall, where we dodderers could don slippers, shuffle in climate controlled conditions, and worry that we were being overtaken by the outrageous fungus, growing between the floor tiles, which was feeding on our rotting trouser cuffs.

That is what they intended, but it is anything but how things turned out. For in their youthful arrogance they failed to factor in the unfactorable: spontaneous, intersubjective insight and rebellion. They didn't take history seriously. They didn't bother to wonder, "How did everyone in France know what to do at the same time in different places in May '68?" If they had bothered to so wonder, they might have feared that we would see a similarity between our present and something in our past. Weren't these colonies rather like the old networks of our countercultural past? The Haight to Santa Barbara to the Strip to Taos to Boulder to Madison to the Village? We flowed with perfect freedom, hitching along the unsuspected circuitry, doing our impression of the artist as a young electron.

So one morning we got out of our beds like Dracula's sleepwalking devotees, except that what called to us wasn't the Count, but the deep darkness under his cape, called Emptiness, another name for total openness of possibility. It was thrilling to be so multiplied, to have won a revolution before we'd even eaten our breakfast.

Looky here: there's your last laugh. Ha! We never succeeded in literally making a revolution, but when it was least expected of us we won it anyway. In the colonies at Elko and Wallawalla and Needles and Manzanar and Kalamazoo, we ate our canned grapefruit sections knowing we'd won. At first, it was nothing dramatic. We exchanged a look, giggled. But even that about drove our attendants crazy. "Why are they smiling? What's happened?"

We'd become superconductors was what happened, buddy. Soon they saw the evidence: a resident from the Boise colony trades places mysteriously with one from Fort Wayne. (Never mind how we did it, that's top secret. Imagine a Star Trek transporter.) Then we hot-wired Boca Raton and switched the entire colony with that in Murfreesboro. This wasn't utopia, it was an even more desirable atopia. We weren't no place, just no particular place. We played. We blew all the circuit breakers. We were cute again and irrepressible.

One time, I hitched into Omaha ("hitching" we called our new zero-gravity, free-circuit, space-time continuum, colony hopping) when they gathered us all into a room. That in itself nearly exhausted their ability to restrict us. It was like gathering ectoplasm. We were slippery as spirit, a jolt of juice, pure conjunction, exactly music. They asked who we were.

"We are word people," we suggested. Truly, a sort of phosphorescence of language prevailed. So they called the Special Tactical Force for words. But by the time they arrived, we were machine people. We were informed that there was a social prohibition on metamorphosis, then someone was dispatched to fetch the Machine Mounties. Meanwhile, the interrogation proceeded:

"How did you get here?"

"Where are the snows of yesteryear?" we replied.

"What kind of machine are you?"

"Is this an orchard?" we asked.

"Are you implying that you grew here?"

"What do elevators do?" we queried.

"Are you being sarcastic?"

"Are you old enough to remember private certitude?"

This interrogation was more dangerous than it might seem to you because the temptation to know the answers to questions is great even at an age when you've forgotten everything. For example, the answer implicit within these questions was "death" (our death), so it was important to provide not merely answers to different questions, but questions to different answers. Fortunately, all our strategies were blessed by the Dukes of Irony, a gang of supersensible street toughs. Even so, the questions we were asked might have done us in if our interrogators had understood that whether we were word people or machine people was of very little consequence, for words and machines are the same thing. Only the Money Cop understands this, and of him we lived in fear.

Once, a few gray-hairs and I had been burning up the grapevine between Mo-town and Tulsa. During the last twenty-four hours we'd coauthored an historical novel about one of the lives Lenin didn't live (in which he said "have a party" not "join the Party"); we'd assembled a full-scale jigsaw puzzle of Montana on top of Nebraska and brought interstate commerce to a standstill; and we'd completed a quilt in which each frame from Kubrick's *A Clockwork Orange* was represented in an embroidered square. It was a big quilt. Anyhow, we'd just come pouring through an outlet in the Tulsa colony when—oops—there he was, the Money Cop. He thought money was a universal equivalent. Real old-fashioned. Of course, he was wrong; a thing may share an identity with everything else, but that thing is not money. Nonetheless, his delusion made him dangerous.

He sat in a Victorian gentleman's armchair, a pearly cane before him, looking like Sidney Greenstreet.

I said, "Wait a minute. I've seen this movie."

"Oh ho ho," he laughed, "please, Miss Alice...it is Miss Alice, isn't it?...sit down. I want to have a chat with you."

My granny cohorts split. They knew a heavy scene when they saw one.

"Don't tell me, I know already. You're going to offer me a job. Well, you can take your job and...."

"Now, now. Not so fast." He turned to a butler-chap at his side. "Guano, offer Miss Alice a cigar. Havana's finest, Miss Alice. The immortal Senor Castro sells them to me. See? Guevara Supremo."

"Let me clarify my purpose. I'm not going to offer you just any job, Miss Alice. I'm offering back your job with Romper Room."

"Romper Room?" I was stunned. "With all the little children in...."

"Yes...in chains yearning to be free. Perhaps you can free them yet, Miss Alice. If you'll just sign this contract."

I gave it a quick look. "A million dollars a day!"

"A mere token. Of course, a million dollars isn't what it used to be, but what is?"

He knocked the ash from his cigar onto a priceless Persian carpet. He made the cigar glow like the sun. I felt faint. I was answering his questions, I couldn't help myself.

"Will I have an expense account?"

"To be sure. Well, we can see to the trivialities of the contract later. Guano, help Miss Alice to the studio, please. I believe the children are waiting."

I was taken by the arm and led through a stage door. But it wasn't Romper Room. It was the Howdy Doody show. There was the Peanut Gallery. Betrayed! There was cheering settling down like soot, and an odd applause that seeped from dismembered arms, legs, and torsos, which flopped like fish on the bleachers. Blood and a colorful holiday assortment of gore cascaded down the risers.

Quick-like, I detached the flashing red bulb from a demented clown's nose and made a dive for the socket. I hit the surge with a jolt, joined the current in midstream and made tracks for the colony in Minneapolis. Behind me I could hear the Money Cop's enormous laugh. He was hollow but tenacious. Tough in the way that white men are tough. Of course, we'd have to deal with his fat ass again.

But when that time came, we'd be ready. Though we are now old, we are close to that place where the world worlds in availability. We'll get there if we live long enough. And if we don't live long enough, well, there is always the next time through the Great Wringer. But at least for the time being we've ceased to clobber the world with our Intentions, as if it were a bad dog that just won't stay down, down. But neither do we let it muddy us with its heavy paws. Instead, we "put on the dog," as it were.

Remember John Lennon

Everybody of my generation has the same memory. We were twelve or thirteen or we were twenty-one, for that matter, and we were going to be veterinarians or we were, like Ringo, going to own a hairdresser's parlor. We walked into the record store and saw the cover of *Sgt. Pepper's Lonely Hearts Club Band.* We thought together, "Life can be other than it has been."

This experience is the phenomenal moment of our generation's Ought. The fact that yippies became yuppies changes that Ought no whit. Every generation has similar opportunities. Our cumulative failure to understand and claim our opportunities is the large part of our poverty.

ECSTASY

"Instant karma's gonna get you."

—John Lennon

The Amazing Hypnagogic Man

I make this, my final log entry, in unimaginable fatigue but not despair.

No, not despair.

But of course I'm not writing this at all! That's the very shock of my discovery.

As I form these letters, in the old style, pen in hand, I see dried snot on the back of my hand where I've wiped it.

Just like when I was a runny-nosed boy.

That trace indicates that even if I don't exist, there is still something that we can call human.

But what word does the glazed snot spell?

My research into the principle of Dependent Origination (a project proceeding in many countries under the auspices of the United Nations Commission on Perdurable Bodies) had until recently followed only the most conventional lines of inquiry.

Our research question had been sharply, if also politically, focused: when matter is considered dynamically and the elements of mind are exterritorialized, is there a difference between matter and mind?

Obviously, the purpose of our inquiry had been skewed by Eastern Bloc countries who had a considerable propagandistic benefit to reap from discovering that in fact mind and matter are one.

Both are forces.

One knows how fragile the global economy of mind has grown.

At first American representatives were inclined to withdraw all support from this project, however sullied such a gesture would leave our reputation for fair-minded scientific investigation.

But I was able to convince our delegation, with a dramatic eleventh-hour telegram, that my unbelievable good fortune in research materials should not be wasted.

With what fate had provided me, I argued, I could spoil the smug, insidious purposes of the Eastern bloc technicians.

Yes, materials had fallen into my lap.

Like the brains of the President had fallen out of his head and into Jackie's white lap.

The decapitated head of Sonja McCaskie, blonde ski star, murdered by eighteen-year-old Tommy Bean.

It was mine to decipher.

The fractured skull of a baby beaten by a boy of four.

All names withheld.

The head and brain of a thalidomide fetus.

A little walnut of crenulated possibility.

The enlarged and unexpectedly complex cranial matter of trout killed by malathion, for whom it was possible to imagine that in their brook a last moment awareness grew (beyond all bounds of fish-thought) that ultimate reality is unutterable but can be felt.

Was it possible that malathion had made the fish Romantics?

This should not be considered strange, for don't the peyote eating brujos of the American southwest precisely poison themselves into mystic vision?

Don't drugs poison them into being something more than human?

159

Because it would have been wrong to waste these opportunities, I was instructed by the secretary of our delegation to proceed with my studies.

I am told that that unanticipated decision alone, and fear of what we might have up our capable sleeves, nearly caused the Soviet delegation to withdraw its support for the U.N. inquiry.

Cooler heads prevailed in the Kremlin, but in Cambodia Buddhist monks revisited anxiety for the first time in years.

But my good fortune knew no bounds.

Just when I had settled in to parse the tangled, splendid messages of my specimens, fate toppled another on me that would cause me to forget even the incisive crannies of a murdered ski star's skull, as if it were no more valuable than a ball of dust brought up from beneath the bed.

It seems that excavators, preparing the site of a housing development, working in a marsh area on the north-east side of the San Francisco Bay, discovered the perfectly preserved corpse of a human body, perhaps as much as a hundred years old, mummified within a peat bog.

The body was mine, the corrugated brain was mine if I wanted it.

I signed out the Institute's Ford Ranchero and drove to the site.

Waving my credentials before the stunned machine operators, encouraging the on-site engineer to sniff the hot plastic of my ID, I was allowed to walk down through the flattened reed beds to a shallow depression, roughly scraped by a dozer's behemoth blade, to the little paleomammalian grave.

When they threw back the rough tarp, I was astonished to see that it was not the bent Indian ancient I expected, but the noble and erect frame of a European, his stylish turn-of-the-century apparel preserved thread-for-thread by the smothering peat.

His flesh too was perfectly preserved, although its tone was that of those dried apple figures grandmothers sell at roadside craft shops.

And he was mine.

"Load him up, fellows," I instructed.

Back in my private study—there was no chance that I would share him with the quaking fingers of my invidious colleagues—I experienced a guilty excitement.

I felt like a pederast who has smuggled a brown native boy into the country and who in a moment will be able to give his imagination free play.

But when the teeth of my bone saw first bit into his brow, I was granted a satisfaction that convinced me that mere clumsy sex would mean nothing to me from that moment forward.

There's a difference between perversion and enlightenment, is there not?

With his cranial cap removed, neat as a beanie, I saw his brain—beyond my most drunken hopes—utterly whole, complete in every part, his pons and medulla as available and perfectly defined as the fingers on my hand.

One of the enduring riddles of Perdurable Body research is the question of the relationship of phenomenology to brain correlates.

Although dead, and thus theoretically beyond the thrashing phenomenal, finding this antique husk opened up the possibility of an evolutionary perspective, which fit my longtime assumption that none of the answers to the significant brain puzzles were extraphysical, and least of all were they supernatural.

At the very most, I had persistently argued, these answers might be subcortical in nature, although even that was unlikely.

Imagine, therefore, my amazement when the probe of my electrical interference instrument—brought to bear only on a whim—produced a measurable thalamic discharge!

Not only was this gypsy whole, present in detail, there was now reason to think his nervous system was capable of carrying a current!

I had inadvertently hot-wired the transient electrical potentials of this baggage.

I began to suspect he required a name.

Baptism was not out of the question.

I called him Vito Bliss after my old friend Bliss Perry.

Relevantly, similar cases have been described by my Harvard mentor, Professor Schnittmuller.

If you doubt what I am here describing, please recall your own amazement at the antics of pickled frogs when once the alligator clips and DC battery were connected to their nimble haunches.

You see, it is possible that what I describe is more than real.

For the first few days of my investigation, I steered clear of further electrical probing and examined his other tissues.

More like what I had expected, I found only an enfeebled tonicity.

One day—a Wednesday or Thursday, I don't know, what difference does it make?—I returned to my probing.

At first, nothing.

But when I burrowed to his pineal gland—the mystic Third Eye in the Vedic tradition—I thought that I heard something.

A fluttering of dry, colorful leaves.

Perhaps the smell of rose petals.

It was his parched tongue, trembling in his mouth.

Carefully, oh so very carefully, I inserted between his grey lips a surgical instrument—a thin dull blade like an aluminum tongue depressor—and opened his mouth.

Silence.

I probed again to the spiritual seat, the pineal gland, which sits in haughty isolation like a caduceus wand at the origin of the spinal cord.

Suddenly my acrid Vito muttered, "Knife, butcher, you are a butcher in a butchery, truly this is a massacre, don't go butchering take measurements."

I was not frightened, oh my reader.

I did not run from the room.

Little tears came to my eyes.

I bent over him reverentially and kissed his sweet lips.

Eventually I was forced to conclude that Vito was neither dead nor alive, but that his suffocating plunge into his boggy grave had obliged a kind of half-sleep upon him.

It is what we in the brain business, we who have the enigmas of Dependent Origination to resolve, call a hypnagogic state.

Hypnagogia is no alien experience; it is that lurid, hopeful time just before sleep when lights, patterns, faces, new mixtures of possibility swim before our eyes like a world of a deeper wakefulness.

It can also be, one admits, that horrid instant in which we awake to wonder who has placed a corpse (in reality, the sleeping body of wife or husband) in one's bed.

In my judgement, the hypnagogic state is simply the ability to perceive all of the electrical activities in one's body: the spinning beauty of electrons nakedly displayed; memory flowing from its briar of cortical ganglia; the energy of one's body interfacing with the energy of the whole human record.

With my electrode and electro-corticography devices, I worked day and night for months mapping out the mind's terrain, but I was never afraid, because I am finally an honest man, to extend that line beyond the pale.

In short, I was not afraid to connect a childhood memory of

music, say, to something that had hitherto been described only in the behavior of a dwarf nebula or the conduct of an infinitely hot and dense dot.

Ordinarily, my probe elicited limited memories.

"Yes, Doctor! Yes, Doctor! Now I hear people laughing—my friends—in San Francisco!"

Or, "I taste the delicate lemon cake! It's on my tongue now!"

However, if I carefully related my proddings, I could occasionally piece together an entire narrative.

Like: "I was very fond of my older sister when I was a boy. Once, for a mean joke, my younger sister woke me from deep sleep and told me my older sister was dead! I cried and sobbed until my sister herself was alarmed. But when she brought my older sister to me, to ease my fear, the sight of her only increased my confusion and terror. The next day, inconsolable over her absence, her presence, I lapsed into convulsions."

To hear this and then look at his face like a dried orange rind was indescribably sad.

I understood then why Heraclitus, the august philosopher of flux, was called the Weeping Philosopher.

But the very worst was when my probing produced the idea that he was "far away from himself" and he would claim to be crying, although his face with the cap of his skull so adroitly removed showed no sign of it.

Curiously, once in a while he would claim experiences he could not imaginably have had in one selfsame life.

He spoke of being a young girl in the entourage of Empress Elizabeth of Austro-Hungary.

He spoke of working for a Berlitz school in Zurich.

He had been a Swedish freethinker in Minnesota.

A Hottentot.

The leader of the Boxer Rebellion.

Coconspirator in the Babylonian Captivity.

Believe me, ordinarily no subject of mine gets away with such drivel, but in his condition I could take it at face value or not at all.

And, I confess, I never considered halting or even pausing in my explorations.

I'd become dependent upon the readouts, the charts, the gentle terrains which I mapped with pencil and caliper.

How could I deny myself the opportunity of being the only intellect in our world with daily, matter-of-fact access to the Beyond?

And so I keep him at my side, bubbling like a thick stew at a constant simmer.

Of course, I long ago abandoned the idea of using my discoveries for the benefit of the United Nations inquiry into Perdurable Bodies.

I've turned in everything in my possession even remotely resembling a credential.

It is clear to me that my findings could only provide comfort for those my country has long called enemy, besides which I lack the self-certainty I would need to survive Ambassador Adlai Stevenson's accusations of betrayal and high treason.

But who knows? Perhaps I will eventually slough the patriot's skin.

As the great Schnittmuller used to scold, "Your precious America is just another political state, and no state is capable of intent, beneficent or otherwise. But even the simplest human mind can intend galaxies!"

Imagine what the brilliant Schnittmuller would have made of the evidence dear Vito supplies!

Whatever the case, my walleyed companion with his buzz-cut

skull, his hippocampus prickly with electrical conductors like a farfetched porcupine, he is my best friend.

Each night when he sings me to sleep, I realize what a difference he has made in my life.

His own example has convinced me that I could not imaginably exist and I am infinitely grateful for that insight.

After all, if Vito is simply a participant in a universal brew, if even severe Vito is no more than energy percolating, and yet he is to my eye or to any objective eye infinitely more plausible than myself, distinctly more real, then how could I imaginably be?

You know, part of the charm of the old brain, the so-called reptilian brain, drooping from the limbic duct-work like gonads, is that it is unable to tell the difference between inside and outside.

"A funny taste in my mouth of the sun," whispers my Vito.

Lovely. Quite, quite lovely.

Some Disease

When I was growing up, I rarely left the limits of San Lorenzo. My life was a round of public schooling and vacations spent playing baseball at local parks. However, I do recall that my father and I occasionally drove across the San Mateo Bridge and up the Bay Shore Freeway to Candlestick Park to see the San Francisco Giants play. What I remember most clearly of that trip is the marshy, black land, just before the bridge, fringing the bay itself. You know, the stuff that Caruso lost his shoe to. I remember its not-altogether-fishy smell of rot. By which I mean a rot that not even the most miserable version of decomposing sea life could account for. Immediately beside this murk were salt ponds—another sensory jolt for a prefab boy of the suburbs. In the ponds the Leslie Salt Company evaporated saline bay water for usable salt which was then harvested and piled in pulsing, granulated mountains. But what colors the ponds produced! Iridescent purples, pinks, weird reds. Really, the only thing I'd ever seen like it was on a fish. You know the experience. You're fishing and your dad hands you a bluegill to torment, but when you put it down you notice how the few scales clinging to your hand catch the light in a wild way. We'd call it psychedelic in just a few years.

The association of salt ponds and fish always made sense to me, although there were no bluegills in the gritty bay. The association also confused me into thinking that it was the ponds causing the local stink. It may in fact have been the ponds causing the stink, but certainly not because of anything having to do with fish.

Just so.

The founding father of the south bay salt business was a man named O. E. Oliver. He was a pioneer in the area (never mind that the Ohlone people had been there for several thousand years). That is, he was one of the first whites to figure a way of obliging the land to spit up a profit (money being the crucial incommensurability between Native Americans and Europeans). However, my purpose isn't to beat poor O. E. Oliver over the head with the club of money's "false universality." But neither do I mean to say that Oliver was innocent of its heap powerful medicine. He understood money's alchemical magic plenty-good. For instance, he used to shoot ducks on the bay, sell them and buy books with the money. "This is like getting these things for nothing, and the sport besides," he said. But, as I say, my purpose here isn't to find him, like old Shylock, to be yet another master of translating flesh into gold. I'm more interested in taking out my pocketknife in order to cut into him, a little speculative incision, just to see if he'll bleed.

January 24, 1908—I was home for two weeks attending to Ernest and his typhoid fever. Took the nurse to the depot today. We fumigated the sickroom and the bathroom today with sulphur.

Oliver had a wife, Lottie, and two sons, Ernest and Roy, and they lived in a modest bay-side estate near old San Lorenzo. Most days

Oliver worked on his salt business—planning buildings, expand-ing ponds, meeting with sales representatives—or he travelled by ferry to San Francisco to talk with his banker about investing his profits. But 1908 was not a routine year for him "on account of Ernest being sick." His son's illness required a lot of anxious work that seems to us now strange and frightening. Remember, typhoid was a "communicable" disease. But it wasn't chatty. It could kill. So each week Oliver would have to fumigate rooms with sulphur, wash clothes and blankets from the sickroom, take apart mattresses and wash the hair in suds and carbolic acid and set it all out in the sun to dry.

But his most important project was the tent. The tent in the yard. The yard outside the house and therefore beyond the pall.of disease.

One morning in early March, Oliver, his second son, Roy, and "the Japanese" (as they called Seiji, their hired hand) got to work on the tent, scraping off and leveling a foundation. The Japanese was particularly helpful and Oliver admired the way he worked with the gravel, the way he smoothed it out. His hands really seemed to know the little round rocks. No wonder they were such good gardeners, he thought. Something racial no doubt. Then they went out to the lumber shed and selected good, straight 4x8 redwood beams for the foundation. Beautiful grain, color of clay, almost indifferent to moisture. But it was some work getting the still wet beams to the foundation, Roy being a thin boy and the Japanese being more sensitive than strong.

But they got them there, lined them up good and straight, dug them down in the grit and braced them inside with old yellow pine 2x4. Then the 1x4 flooring on top, driven right into the beams with squared tenpenny nails that Oliver had cast himself. While Oliver cut the planking down to size, over on the sawhorse, the Japanese

169

and Roy lined them up and drove 'em home. Things were going smoothly, and the work felt so good that Oliver had almost lost the guilty feeling that building the tent was equivalent to abandoning Ernest. How would the boy feel about driving his family out of their own house into the yard? But then Oliver looked over at Roy, pounding nails, and noticed that with each stroke of the hammer a blossom of bright blood appeared on the wood just to the left of the nail being driven. It looked as if the wood itself were suffering little eruptions of gore. What in the world could it be? Alarmed, he looked more closely and realized that each blow caused Roy's body to quake and each quake shook loose a droplet of blood from his son's nose.

"Roy! Stop a minute!"

Roy stopped, looked up at his father and wiped at his nose with his shirt sleeve, the cloth already streaked with red and brown.

"What's the matter with your nose?"

"Oh, I've just got a nose bleed, Dad. It's nothing much."

"Well, how did you get that?"

"It happens now and again. I think I've got a pimple in there."

"Pimple?" Oliver said, putting down the saw quickly. "Goddamn, sit down and let me see."

Roy sat obediently on the floorboards he'd just fastened.

Oliver was amazed. What he saw at the back of his son's left nostril was no pimple. Carbuncle, feruncle, pustule, growth, cyst, tumor, sac, capsulelike membrane, pod, tuber, swollen part, bubo, potato, nodule, wartlike excrescence, bean of death, any of those, yes. But pimple, no.

"My god, son. That's no pimple. I'll be damned. Seiji, come here. You ever see anything like this?"

Oliver sat and took his head in his hands as Seiji, the Japanese, looked.

"No, Mr. Oliver. Never see something like that."

"I'll bet not." Oliver got up to look again as if maybe it would be less dramatic from another angle. "How do you breathe with that thing?"

"Sometimes I breathe through my mouth."

"God bless me, I guess you do."

He took his son's head in his hands, kissed his cheek, then ducked back down to confront the menace.

March 2—Ernest is getting along well now but not outside yet—picking up fast in flesh but pulse is too high yet.

March 29—Cut Ernest's hair. Roy is down in bed with measles.

Modern astronomers and physicists, in their commitment to exhaust ignorance, to run it down, in their desire to help others attain profound emptiness, have imagined, discovered and are now in the process of describing what they call "black holes." These masters have not lived their lives like preoccupied children playing with toys in a house that is burning to the ground. No. They have paid attention. They have made contact with the real in their Dream Practice.

But just what is a black hole? It is a star, friends, one of heaven's corpulent bodies, whose gravitational mass has grown so large that nothing can escape its field, not even light pumping its pedals at 186,000 miles per second. So it collapses back upon itself, nested more insidiously than any Chinese box, so that a thimble of it weighs tons.

Of course, scientists—being our kin—at first resisted the wisdom implied in their discoveries. For instance, in 1927, Sir Arthur Eddington said of these collapsing stars, "The message of the companion of Sirius when it was decoded ran: 'I am composed of material 3,000 times denser than anything you have come across; a ton of my material would be a nugget that you could put into a matchbox.' What reply can one make to such a message? The reply which most of us made in 1914 was—'Shut up. Don't talk nonsense.'"

April 14—Put steps on tent-house. Got my car ready and by 11 o'clock we took a trip up to the county infirmary to see Dr. Clark about Roy's nose.

After returning from Dr. Clark's office, Oliver went out into the yard to make final arrangements for the sleeping tent. He assembled the spare maple bedstead, and managed to wrestle the heavy horsehair mattress onto the bed frame without the Japanese's annoying aid. When he left the tent and looked back toward the house, he felt despondent. I mean, he lived it, he inhabited despondency. He did its negative bidding. The house receded, seemed insubstantial and strange, jumped about absurdly because Oliver was too depressed to fix it in one spot with his usually certain gaze. All he could think about was death, corruption and change for the worse. Mutability! You familiar hound!

Suddenly, a razor appeared in his hand. He would do something desperate. He turned back into the tent, climbed up on the bed, reached to the ceiling and slashed a dramatic gash in the canvas. He felt a little better, but he was glad Lottie wasn't watching him. Then, more carefully, he lengthened the sagging gash, straightened it and cut purposeful lines at right angles to it. Another long cut on the far side and a perfect rectangle of cloth fell to the planking. He ran to the house and brought some fine netting back to the tent.

When Lottie came looking for Oliver at dinner time, she found him on his back on a platform, a version of Michelangelo's Sistine patience, sewing the netting into the canvas skylight. She had been concerned about his state of mind—they were all awfully upset about the boys' health—so she came up cautiously to his work.

"Dear, what are you doing?" she inquired.

"I've made a skylight for the tent."

"Why?"

"Can't you see? It will be right over our heads in bed. We can watch the stars at night."

"Oh. That will be nice. But what if it rains?"

"It's not going to rain."

"How do you know it won't rain?"

"It won't rain."

June 13—Ernest down with diptheria and can't go outside our gate until further orders from Board of Health. We are quarantined and house has been fumigated.

A bad day. Even though he understood the need for isolating his son/his disease, Oliver felt leprous, a public threat, something the world would be well-off sloughing. Bold, red quarantine signs prohibited even peddlers who otherwise couldn't be kept away with a shotgun. Even they could imagine the consequences of toting disease to Oakland in their case of gewgaws. Then came the men in the masks, with the pressurized tanks of sulphur, choking clouds of the stuff. How could you not feel that the contempt of the community was focused on you? That you were not a lot different from a pestilent vermin needing extermination? And how did you say, "I'm sorry, I don't know what I did. I agree, this is the sign of a moral failing, but which one? When?" You couldn't call a meeting down to the schoolhouse to clear the air, bare your breast, 'cause no one would come, 'cause that was just the point—to stay away from you!

So Oliver was glad, that night, to be able to surrender, to cease to exert desire, and crawl into the tent and the bed next to his warm and already sleeping wife. He gazed up through the skylight at the multitudinous night. He was looking at that area of the sky where the spiral galaxy NGC 5194 loiters (in the constellation Canes Venatici). Such galaxies contain a brilliant core whose energy source is hotly debated. Of course, Oliver didn't know that. And of course one can't see this galaxy without the aid of something like the five-meter telescope at Mt. Palomar. The sad fact of the matter was that when Oliver took off his glasses, he could just barely see crummy regular stars, let alone that strident beauty, Canes Venatici.

The essence of a black hole is a point, its core, where density becomes infinite and time and space disappear—a "singularity."

Many physicists speculate that what banged big originally was precisely an infinitely dense singularity. "But wherefrom cameth the first singularity?" ask the Thomists among you. Obviously, there's no answering such a question, obscured as it is in the Big Hen House among innumerable, milling, coy chickens and infinite enigmatic eggs. But what if the cosmos were not so much the result of a bang as of a sort of regurgitation? What if the original black hole were a sort of bridge between two universes, our own and an anti-universe, you know, a Hegelian antithesis, a cosmos of the revolutionary proletariat, a place where businessmen can't find jobs and so hang out in parks smoking cigarettes and talking cheap? Thus, in our universe dominated by matter, time flows forward; but in the Siamese cosmos dominated by antimatter, time might flow in the opposite direction. The two universes are constantly moving in and out of each other, one collapsing while its companion, in a fit of revulsion at the sudden proximity of this too-familiar Other, spews it back out (rebirth).

What I particularly like about this image of Being is that when a singularity belches forth a new universe, it is not necessary that the physical laws, constants, gravity, circuitry and that shit should be the same as in this universe. Because after having been squeezed through a knothole, wrung through the cosmic wringer and changed utterly, the new universe would have no memory of what had ruled its predecessor. Rules, argues John Wheeler, "are freshly given for each fresh cycle of the universe."

I don't know about you, but I haven't heard anything that hopeful in a long time.

When I was a kid, I too slept out in the yard, although I wasn't driven there by disease. I just wanted to "camp out." So, I dragged

175

my sleeping bag with the red flannel scenes of cowboys, Indians and three rampaging buffaloes out onto the mattress of crabgrass in my backyard and gazed up into the great corpse of the starlit sky. What I saw there amazed me for five minutes (just long enough to find the Big Dipper) and then put me to sleep. I know the sky is a surreal scene, but at that time I couldn't see it. I was a sorry little realist.

About the only thing that would have impressed me (and it would impress me still) is if I had looked up and seen what Stephen Hawking calls a "naked singularity." What if a singularity had added to it sufficient angular momentum that it was distorted, elongated and thus made "naked," permitting a glimpse of what was inside it? What would we see there? An Event Horizon would snap open, allowing information from within the hole to escape. The rules of probability would become invalid. Causality would no longer apply. Salvador Dali could at last feel comfortable and take a nap. No prediction could be made as to what might come out of the hole. It could be anything "from television sets to busts of Abraham Lincoln" (William Press).

For no good reason, this helps me to understand the time I was sleeping in the back and I got up in the middle of the night and sleepwalked into the house into the living room where the TV emitted its grey noise. I was apparently headed for the front door when my father stopped me.

"Hey Butch, where do you think you're going?"

I woke then and looked at him, but his face failed to cohere. None of the parts fit. His face was, I could see, just a mixture of time, weather and some people. Well, of such an experience I can only say, "One observes and it liberates."

176

June 23, 1908—Ernest died today and will be buried tomorrow.

July 11—Lottie, Roy and I went up to Dr. Cornwall at 631 Van Ness Avenue this morning and we had Roy chloroformed and his tonsils trimmed some and the adenoid cut out of his throat. In about 10 days we are to come back and get the growth cut out of his left nostril.

The night before Roy's nose operation, Oliver couldn't sleep. His wife had managed to cry herself to sleep around midnight. It was all getting very discouraging. Even Oliver's relationship to Lottie seemed threatened. They had pulled together at first, united in comforting each other over Ernest's death, but now, unpredictably, the differences in their grieving were coming between them. Lottie had accused him of not suffering sufficiently. Of not grieving and thus not ever really loving their son. Now if he did anything lifelike, if he tried just to go to work, he was condemned and called guilty by his wife. This, of course, made Oliver terrifically angry. At some level he understood that Lottie's irrationality was just a symptom of her suffering, but he couldn't help resenting it and distancing himself from her. So, after she was asleep, Oliver got out of bed, where he could no longer rest, and went out to the sleeping tent in the yard. Although Ernest and his diseases were gone, the tent remained, an indication of what they expected from the future.

Oliver lay in the tent gazing up at the spectacle the universe made of itself, when suddenly it occurred to me that I had looked at those same stars from the same place during my boyhood campouts. And that I bet we "registered" them in the same way and that they made us both wonder, "Well, where exactly am I?" and I realized that rightly understood I was helping him as he was helping me. I felt ecstatic about this notion.

July 22—Lottie, Roy and I went to Dr. Cornwall's this morning and had Roy's nose operated on—cutting out the growth—was a very painful operation—cocaine didn't do any good, it seemed. The Doctor used knives and scissors and saws and also did some burning. Took about 1/2 hour I guess, filled the nostril up with iodoform gauze when done—sprayed it some also with something.

November 7—I moved the bed out of the tent and into house. Will not live outside any more until next summer. Have slept fine the whole time. I was sleeping so poorly for a month before getting the tent that I was afraid I was going to be down sick with some disease.

One night in the late fall after Ernest's death, O. E. Oliver went out to the tent. It was empty now, and on the next day he planned to take down the canvas so it wouldn't rip in a winter storm. As he stood there, he had a sort of vision. You may recall that those days were sufficiently distant from our own intractable time that such things were possible. Seeing then was more than a kind of technical competence that your body performed. There was insight as well. You know yourself of the story told you by aunt B. of great-grandmother C., the night she received a phone call, 1919 it was, from her brother Virgil in the Dakotas, and he sort of rose before her eyes saying he had just died and wanted only to say, "Good-bye, sweet sister, I did love you!"

Well, Oliver was open to such things, too. The night suddenly flared daylit and he saw some future boy in a Little League uniform smack a fly ball with a fungo. Oliver knew what to do. He'd actually played some ball in Oakland and rooted for Christy Mathewson. He backpedalled, settled under it, tapped his glove (I think he was going to make a basket catch like Willie Mays, the show-off) but then, *mirabile dictu*, the ball became the moon, bright pie-face against the perplexing dark of the sky. Oliver wobbled for a moment in dizzy amazement, as if about to fall face first into understanding. This should have been a moment of great and unexpected joy for him. For even though he did not recognize his bliss as bliss, the play of the bobbing moon was his own energy sporting in space's companionable void, where everything is writ large and evident for myopic us. It would be more to my purpose to leave him there, tangled in our fate, but—truth be told—he reoriented himself quickly. Soon, he was back in the house, at his desk, because, in fact, he had a payroll to get out.

Anyhow, that's the true story of a particularly sad series of events in the life of O. E. Oliver. Or perhaps I should say, as John Faulkner did at the Dallas meeting of the Texas Symposium on Relativistic Astrophysics in 1974, "This is the desire upon which I base my facts."

Still Human

"Is a human cry nothing at all?"

—Paul Gauguin

Sex and Food a Mouthful at a Time

Wanda and Dave were in their backyard, being adored by the compassionate California sun, reclining in redwood recliners. Dave protected his easily burnt nose with one of those green plastic visors you see on Reno card sharps. Actually, it was Wanda's visor, and she hated it when Dave wore it because he used Brylcreem in his hair and it seemed to get the strap greasy in spite of what they told you in commercials. Nonetheless, Dave thought that if he put the visor on first it was his. They had just finished arguing about it, but you know how that get-your-own-goddamned-visor-argument goes. Your life too is notoriously petty.

Anyway, Wanda was finally in a drowsy in-between state, almost dreaming, which was for her the principal pleasure of sunbathing. A previous incarnation flashed before her, then vanished: she was the daughter of a vintner in the Penedes, was courted, had a baby, hated her husband, and died. In the yeasty aftermath of this vision, a very different thought occurred to her. She sat up, squinting, picked up a bottle of Johnson & Johnson's baby oil and spread it on her belly in a way that never failed to excite Dave. Especially exciting was the little puddle in her navel. He actually thought of it as Narcissus' pond, and once he bent down close enough to see the reflection of one hungry eye in it, violent as a belly dancer's ruby. Then Wanda said, in a way that seemed offhand but was really only banal, "Recently, time has been passing so quickly for me."

It wasn't like her to be troubled by such ideas. After all, time's most ferocious implication is death, and Wanda did not often concern herself with death. She had enough to do just keeping Dave's mitts off her belongings. If Dave had been paying attention to what she said, he'd have wondered if there were not some depth to Wanda's character that he hadn't noticed before. But let's be frank, Dave felt only contempt for what Wanda was capable of thinking, although that did nothing to distance him from his need for her as Platinum Goddess of Love. As a consequence, he responded as if the thought had been his own. "You're not concentrating hard enough," he said.

Wanda was confused by Dave's reply, but she was usually puzzled by what he said, because his ideas were almost always unintelligible, or—as in this case—spectacularly oblique, or cogent only in the way that, for example, the idea of Diseases from Space is cogent: it explains a lot, it explains too much, it makes you angry to have to think about. The trouble with Dave was that he had so many ideas, like a colony of ants his brain was, and about as useful. In fact, since settling in the Village, Dave had acquired a reputation as a sort of backyard philosopher, which was fine if you happened to be a backyard. To be fair to him, his comment to

Wanda was not completely random; he'd been thinking about time recently. He'd read in *Popular Mechanics* that the universe had begun, in a big bang, ten billion years ago. So it made sense to him to continue, "You have a point, though. That first ten billion years really went by fast, didn't it?"

Wanda had let his first comment pass, but this second made it clear to her that she was being ridiculed. She jumped up from her lounge, the oil flying from her, and stormed toward the kitchen door, saying, "You really bug me, Bohannon." She growled it. This anger was the real thing. Nonetheless, Dave noticed only the wet smack of her bare feet on the patio concrete and was immediately aroused. He followed her, prepared to pick up his half of a quarrel, but really hoping this whole thing would somehow lead to bed. To hell with time, to hell with their utter incompatibility: he wanted to suck the oil from her toes.

As Dave followed Wanda into the house, there was a moment of unexpected but spectacular violence that he would remember like a lurid Technicolor scene from a slasher movie. Slow motion too. As Wanda rushed toward the kitchen, she heard Dave following, and in trying to slam the sheet metal screen door in his face she accidentally caught its utterly sharp aluminum corner on her ankle which split a minimum four inches of the flesh above the brittle ankle right down to the bone.

"Ahhhh!" she screamed.

"Oh my god, Wanda, darling, are you okay? I thought I saw bone."

"Jesus!"

She sat and turned her leg to look at her ankle. The cut was so clean and the area so shallow that it hadn't begun to bleed yet. And there, sure enough, through the gash peeked a surprising bright hard white.

Dave kneeled at her feet. "My god, I can see the bone. Wait."

"Ouch! What are you doing!"

"I want to see a little more. This is an incredible opportunity."

"I'm going to kill you."

"Look at that!"

Things were calmer that evening, but not concluded. Dave's left eye was nearly swollen shut, but Wanda's leg, at least, was bandaged and had stopped bleeding. She was at the front door with a couple of suitcases.

"David, I'm going home to Roy."

"Roy! When will I hear the end of this Roy? What has he got to do with anything? He's cut out of a cheap Italian opera. I'm sick to death of the very possibility of Roy."

"Well, you won't have to hear about him anymore because there won't be anyone here to say anything about him because I'll be with Roy and not here."

Then she was out the door, giving her head a little toss as she left, her hair a bloody blonde wave behind her.

Dave's comment about "concentration" was based upon a half-understood idea from Einstein that time is dependent upon perception, that it has to do with perspective, both of which imply consciousness. What is time in a cosmos without consciousness? he wondered. So the difference between the twinkle that was the first ten billion years and the present (so often tedious!) suburban moment, post-WW II sunny California, was that now there were a lot of people around paying attention. So, by extension, he theorized, if time seemed to be getting out of control, hurrying away, then it could be slowed down by thinking hard about it. In the other direction, he feared a moment of mass distraction or inattention in which the universe would suddenly rush away, like a river without a source that could flow by in an instant leaving the riverbed dry and a few flopping carp miserable.

It was a hair-trigger universe for a certainty. Precarious as the devil.

But Dave's favorite theory by a mile was the idea that our bodies present themselves for the same reason that stars are present for our amazed study. We resist entropy and collapse, the nihilistic attraction of gravity, because we are capable of metabolizing vegetable and flesh, thus burning/expanding hotly enough to resist becoming that ultimate failure of Being…a BLACK HOLE. Our body then is a post-primordial abyss into which we slough ourselves one cell at a time. Thus, to say body is to say grave. A skin cell is sloughed and plummets into the nothing at the heart of us.

Perhaps a theory of entropy of one kind or another would have helped explain for Wanda her experience while walking over to Roy's place. It was a pretty good hike (especially with two suitcases and in high heels) from the new Del Rey subdivision to the old Village center. She certainly knew the way, but she wasn't paying much attention because she was thinking about the trauma of leaving Dave. He was a sweet man and an inconsiderate jerk who built houses and had funny ideas that enraged and charmed her. But he couldn't keep himself alive, and there would soon no doubt be rumors again about him eating Milk Duds for dinner at the theater. He might even go back to sleeping at the Camp Fire Girl cabin. He'd collapse! But she continued anyway, unwilling to change her mind or seem weak. If she went back, he might think she really cared about him or loved him or something dumb like that. She had to take care of herself first.

Well, she came right up to Roy's door and knocked. But imagine her surprise when the door was answered by Dave! The obvious things ran through her mind:

* she'd walked in a circle, made absentminded by her high emotions;

* she'd become confused by the tract home redundancy of every village house and entered the wrong one;

* Dave had run ahead and made himself free with Roy's home in the way he had many times in the past;

* she had hiked into the truth that the space-time continuum is curved and that its warp leads full circle.

Whatever the case, her feelings gave way at that point and she fell sobbing onto sobbing Dave and after a lot of wet smooching they concluded their very stressful day in bed.

Later, they talked.

"You know, you really hurt me this morning," said Wanda. "There I was cut badly and you made it worse by pulling at it so you could see the bone. What about my pain? Didn't that mean anything to you? Isn't that more important than your stupid curiosity?"

"I'm sorry, dear. I was wrong. And I'll try to make it up to you."

So saying, he pulled back the covers and revealed his own favorite affront to gravity, which bobbed its little head like a Christmas puppy, but which he intended whimsically as his "bone."

"Indulge your own curiosity to the full, sweetheart."

They laughed at the joke then hugged and kissed in a way that was not politically correct but was, I hope you will take my word for it, convincing.

185

The Idea Which Reality Seeks

The great Comanche chief, Quanah Parker, once testified during a session of the Oklahoma State Legislature. At issue was whether or not the little spineless cactus, peyote, should be made illegal, even to those Indian tribes which used it as an element in religious rituals.

"I do not think this Oklahoma legislature should interfere with a man's religion," Parker said. "Also these people should be allowed to retain their health restorer."

Great though Parker was, our real interest here is in the next witness, Joe Green, a shaman, a peyotist and a deacon in the Episcopalian Church. Indian rights advocates felt that his unusual authority in the white man's church would make him a persuasive voice in this hearing. The only thing they feared was that Joe Green also had a reputation as a bit of a wild man, what the Indians called a Trickster.

Green approached the testimony table. He was short and stocky with close-cropped greying hair. His clothing was casual and western style. He looked like a ranch hand wearing his cleanest shirt and fanciest string tie. Immediately after sitting, Green waved the state's legal counsel over to him and said, in a whisper, "You know, supernatural benefits can be expected by those who have homosexual relations with a holy person like myself." He gave him a little conspiratorial wink.

The counsel raised his head in horror.

"Is there a problem, counsel?"

"N-no, sir," he replied. But he was shaken, and he had lost control of the interrogation before he had even begun. Later, he would defend his poor performance by repeating what Joe Green had said, to which claim his superiors reacted with skepticism and thinly veiled disdain for the depths to which some lawyers sink in order to protect their own interests. It is not at all coincidental that not long afterward, this lawyer began to hit the cognac in a way that would make it certain that he would not see his fifty-second birthday.

On the night of the lawyer's death, the warrior Joe Green had a vision of his whimpering end and, frowning, added another honky tonsure to his war belt.

Joe Green's mystic skills, his speculative powers, displayed themselves when he was very young. Once, when he was but ten years old, he was taken to the home of an uncle who was said to be near death. He had the "witch sickness" that had been shot into him by a sorcerer. When Joe went up to kiss his uncle farewell, he bent not to his face or lips but to the top of his head and fastened his mouth rudely. His relatives were shocked, the uncle writhed, but they couldn't unfasten the boy.

Moments later, he lifted of his own will, his mouth covered with blood and dark hair. His mother was embarrassed and was about to scold him when he produced at his lips a small rock crystal which had passed from the patient to the new shaman's mouth through the top of the patient's head.

His uncle slept peacefully, his errant soul returned.

Not many years after, Joe met a Crow Indian, Frank Takes Gun, the president of the Native American Church. Frank was a sort of peddler, a traveling sales Indian, who had but one commodity: a little spineless cactus with a root like a carrot and a spongy green crown of about an inch or so in height.

"So what do you do with this, Frank Takes Gun?"

187

"You eat it and get smart."

"Oh. In that case I'll buy some."

Thus was Joe begun on the same path of sight that Vedic seers trod when they drank the splendid tea, soma, distillation of the psychotropic drug amanita muscaria. The purpose then was visualization wherein the meditator actually produced an alternative reality for himself: a reality as real (and as unreal) as the one we know, and a reality, above all, that he could share with others. Joe Green's purposes were no less generous. He was so generous with his own constructions that he had room for the constructions of others. He became a pan-cultural assimilator of religions. He became a sort of spiritual hermit crab who resents having to choose one shell in which to live, so chooses them all, stacks them one on top of the other, like the Apartment Complex of Babel. In 1913 he went so far as to become a deacon in the Episcopalian church, diocese of Sparks, Nevada. He was particularly happy about this because he loved the little spiky hats that deacons wore during ceremonies.

Back at the Oklahoma State Legislature's hearings into drug use, the legislative counsel was about to begin his questioning when Joe Green interrupted.

"Would it be inappropriate for me to say a prayer before we start?"

"Of course it would be inappropriate," the functionary said, still a little pissed about Joe's homo ploy, "This body is in official session and every minute costs the taxpayers of this state real money."

"Mr. Counsel," the committee chair inserted, perhaps feeling some of the contempt for such guys that the rest of us feel, "I see no harm in allowing Mr. Green to say a short prayer before beginning his testimony. We don't wish to offend our Episcopalian friends."

"Thank you, Mr. Chairman," said Joe, bowing.

Then he stood, turned to the audience in the hearing room, closed his eyes and raised his arms. "Dear God and Jesus and Mary and Peyote, bless the Indians everywhere in America."

He continued, arms raised, waggling his fingers in a slightly theatrical manner, "We know that we learn by eating peyote and that all things are made known to us by eating this divine plant that you have created for each and every one of us.

"Especially make us strong to resist temptation when someone offers us whiskey, for whiskey makes people stupid as our white brothers can attest."

So saying, he sat.

You can imagine how the remainder of this session went. For example, when the counsel asked, "Mr. Green, don't you think it's important for the government to fight the dope trade which is victimizing our citizens, including the Indians?"

Joe replied, "This legislature hasn't been to a peyote meeting and it hasn't eaten peyote and it doesn't know anything about it. As your own scientists have testified, it's not a narcotic and it isn't habit-forming. But more important, the peyote plant is of divine origin and has a similar relation to the Indians—most of whom can't read—as does the Holy Bible to the white man. Therefore, this legislation you propose would make you Bible burners."

That was his most polite answer. But then counsel asked, "Isn't it true that the use of peyote has spread to a number of communities of negroes?"

At that, Joe's voice registered an alarming authority. "Members of the legislature, peyote teaches very specifically that we ought to have compassion toward others. To achieve that, he recommends that we imagine that every person, at one time or another, has been our mother. If counsel could believe that these Negroes to whom he refers have all been his mother in one life or another, he might not worry in the way that he does that Skillful Peyote could harm them."

Then he moved rapidly to a conclusion. "Your decision today, Oklahoma, doesn't matter. Spirit has its own destiny. It will make its way whatever we do. Spirit is the Idea that reality seeks. What we ought to be doing is enjoying the spectacle, because Wisdom's progress is beautiful. It is with this viewing that peyote helps. Peyote is like your astronomer's telescope. Spirit provides it for us so that we humans, some of us blind as moles, can see what goes on right under our noses."

Finally, he thanked everybody kindly for their interest in his opinions and left.

In spite of Quanah Parker's brilliant ability to reason with whites and Joe Green's passionate dramatizing of the real situation, when the legislature was done with its legislating, the law read as follows:

"We admonish you and summon you to obedience under penalty of anathema and other pecuniary and corporal penalties within our discretion...."

Actually, no, that's a lie. That prohibition was the fancywork of the City of Mexico, 1620. Oklahoma's law really read, "It is hereby declared in the police and sovereign power of the State of Oklahoma that the use of anhalonium, or peyote, within the state is dangerous to the life, liberty, property, health, education, morals and safety of the people of Oklahoma."

One more Joe Green anecdote.

As we have seen, Joe was a good example of the fact that people who believe in many spiritual beings are not opposed to accepting new ones. Only once was his ability to assimilate really challenged. I have heard that at one time, while travelling in New Mexico, he came upon a meeting of the Penitentes, Los Hermanos Penitentes. The Penitentes were an extreme hybrid cult of Roman Catholic Indians and Mexicans, thriving in a remote area of the American Southwest, who had taken an emphatically personal understanding of Christ's martyrdom. Their practice had been developing for nearly a century detached from any orthodoxy. Apparently, their principles had been established in the 18th century by a wandering zealot of the Jesuit order, Father Jorge Violet. After Violet's death, the enclave developed in monstrous isolation until the conclusion of the Mexican American War and the districting of New Mexico in 1848. In general terms, their worship was founded on self-torture. They practiced bloody flagellation, lengthy marches with the "Death Cart" and spectacularly crude reenactments of the crucifixion of Jesus. They were also notoriously hostile to suggestions that there was anything aberrant about their form of worship.

So, one day Joe was moving through their part of the world, hitching in a rancher's old Ford pickup truck, when he saw a dazzling commotion. A crowd of fifty or more people were carrying this enormous doll, a figure of the Christ carved from the trunk of a tree. They were laughing or shouting or cursing or wailing, it wasn't quite clear, and heading toward a squat little building (their odious place of worship, as it turned out, called a morada.) Well, it was just the sort of curiosity that Joe Green was incapable of resisting, so he had the driver stop and let him out.

"Shoot, you gon' get out here?"

"Sure."

"Shoot, you're a crazy man."

"How's that?"

"You'll find out. Hope you got a recipe for cactus salve on you."

By the time Joe reached the morada, the celebrants were all inside. He pulled back the crude board and cowhide door and peered into the pitchy dark. The air was all a moaning, and the heat and stink were palpable. When his eyes had adjusted, he saw that the entire audience had turned to him with expressions not a bit friendly on their faces.

A tall, authoritative man walked through a narrow aisle to Joe and, reaching him, signalled to the rest that the ceremony should proceed. Immediately, the moaning and chanting resumed. Meanwhile, the man questioned Joe.

"What do you want?"

"I just thought I'd join you," said Joe. "I'm a religious man myself."

"What tribe do you belong to?"

"Crow."

"And what makes you think a Crow will like the religion of the Brotherhood?"

"I've never yet met a form of the spirit I haven't liked."

At that the man smiled so that the yellow stumps of his teeth sort of ignited like a jack-o'-lantern with a candle too large and so hot that you know that the pumpkin head will be but a browned-out skull by the morning. This frightened Joe more than a little not because of the innate scariness of the sight, but because he knew it was a bad omen when he started seeing things in terms of white man clichés.

Shortly, the stinking morada was nearly unbearable. The smoke from the coals, the sweat and heat of the gathered bodies was overwhelming. To Joe's amazement, though, the folks seemed to like it. Many of them claimed to be seeing spirits in the air. It was true, the smoke was thick and the brain was in the squeeze of these poisonous fumes so that it was almost impossible not to see things. Joe thought he could get the hang of it, but he wasn't sure he wanted to.

"Hey, Peyote, I've met your cousin and he has some peculiar ways."

Just before Joe thought he couldn't take another moment, just before he launched himself out the door into some breathable air, the ceremony reached its climax. They all removed their shirts with a colossal shrug and began a chant which they punctuated with violent lashings of the back before them with tough bundles of grasses. Obviously, that left the hintermost backs unflayed, a problem which they corrected by rotating from the front rows. Soon the flagellants seemed to flow. They had all the precision of a marching band at halftime but were even more gruesome.

Finally, they brought a heavy, bosomy older woman to the front and strapped her at the wrists and ankles straight up against the enormous T-shaped Cristo which Joe had earlier seen them lugging toward the morada. Her weight was held by a narrow plank jutting from the statue's crotch like guess what. It looked obscene.

"NOW SHE IS TRULY THE BRIDE OF CHRIST!"

Then the entire congregation flowed past her, each member pausing to deliver a single worshipful stroke to her back before filing out of the morada and proceeding down to a spring for a sobering group bath.

Joe stayed behind and went up to the suffering woman. The welts on her back formed patterns and complexities as convincing as any other experience of the world. No doubt, there was the possibility for a kind of awe in it.

He took a pouch of powder from his belt and, adding his own

spit to it, created a plaster for her back. As he ran his finger along the worst gashes they seemed to close like zippers. When he kissed her wounds a dense steam rose into the air.

"Listen, Peyote," Joe muttered, "what if reality seeks the wrong idea?"

Emptiness Is Empty Too

Paris, 1873

A slim, earnest young man trudged by the Café Guerbois, Avenue de Clichy, reading Baudelaire's *Les Fleurs du Mal* which he held in his left hand. The index finger of his right hand was in his nose up to the first knuckle.

From a window table inside the Guerbois, Edgar Degas, Emile Zola, Louis Duranty and their chief, Edouard Manet, watched his risky progress.

"Observe the human beast busy with itself," said Degas.

"Is that Realism, Zola?"

"No, I call that Cretinism."

"But isn't that our little friend Blanche?"

"Great gods it is. I didn't recognize him with the silly hat."

"And he hasn't always his digit in his nose."

"No, not every moment of the day. But I admit, he wears his pick-nez nicely."

"Oh no, he's seen us."

Blanche entered and walked in high intellectual spirits to the table of the notorious group of Manet, outcasts of the Salon. Blanche was a great admirer of the new style. He too was a painter, poet and composer. He was a supporter of the New. If he were a rich man, he would be their champion. He would buy their work and write articles praising them and invite them into the best society. But at that moment, something unbelievable had caught his imagination.

He walked up to the table of Manet indicating the back of his left hand.

"Look, friends, I wiped my nose with the back of my hand a few moments ago and it crystallized in the cold. But wonderfully it seems to have crystallized in the form of a letter, perhaps a word. Take a look, what do you think it says?"

"Not too close for me, Blanche."

"Hmmmm, yes, fine academic French at that," observed Manet. "I think it spells *pomme-tête.*"

"No!" exclaimed Blanche, "You jest! That's far too many letters. I think that's an 'l' and that an 'a' or 'e'."

Degas decided to take a closer look.

"It says 'da'."

Blanche was surprised. "M. Degas, you are too sure of your judgements. It may be 'da,' but if it is, what sense does it make? Why would the Imagination send 'da'? Dada. That's baby talk!"

"True, true," Degas rejoined. "And perhaps the next great thing. But tell me, I've been meaning to ask you, what do you believe is the purpose of stupid people?"

"The purpose?"

"Yes, why do we have them? Why are they needed in the grand order of things?"

"Well, we shouldn't assume everything is for a reason or a purpose, as you say. That's antique thinking. But I can say that although there may be stupid people among us, no one is smart enough. In that sense we are all perhaps what you call stupid."

"*Touché*, Edgar."

"How about sycophants, then?"

"Yes, oh learned Athenian. Tell us of sycophants."

"Sycophants. What is a sycophant?"

"A toady, young sir. Someone who plays to his betters for the sake of adding some gloss to his own otherwise tawdry coat."

"It has to do with coats?"

"A bootlicker, Blanche. Get on with it."

"Oh." Blanche considered this tough nut. "If there is a real distinction here, if we are talking about something beyond simple unkindness or cruelty practiced on those who merely wish to be our friends, then…well, I don't know. I'm not sure that such people exist. How do you recognize them?"

Degas grinned glumly. "Don't worry your head about it, Blanche. Here, drink this Pernod down. That's medicine for artists."

When his own vanity was not at issue, Edouard Manet was a kind man. He pitied the penniless painters around him, wished to help them, and listened patiently to their many plans for fame and greatness. He was also capable of concern for those, like Blanche, who would never make any claim to greatness. For this reason, he returned to the Guerbois early the next day, a little worried about him. He hoped to see Degas and fortunately he was there, looking a bit pasty and pale from the previous evening's excesses. Degas stared out the window over his third cup of coffee.

Manet sat opposite him and got to the point. "Edgar, did you and Blanche make a night of it?"

"Night makes night of itself. It needs no help from me. You wake up in the morning, put on some socks and next thing you know it's dark and you're taking them off."

"Come on, come on. What did you do after you left with Blanche?"

"Is this a question of getting at the essence of life through its significant gestures? For Blanche has significant gestures even if he doesn't intend them."

"Yes, anyway you like, just tell me where you went."

"Montmartre."

"I feared as much."

Degas laughed. "Do you know what Blanche plans to do? He's going to write a poem this winter by taking a walk every evening and wiping his nose on the back of his hand. He figures if the weather remains cool for three more months and he uses both hands he can have a poem of one hundred and eighty words by the spring. He says he'll call it 'Still Human.' You know, sometimes he is very funny. An idiot, but a funny idiot." Degas couldn't stop giggling. "But the funniest thing is he's going to dedicate it to *Mon Ami*, Manet.'

Manet paled, then turned angry. "I don't suppose you had anything to do with that."

"Me? You think I control what pops into his head? I merely mentioned that to have a poem dedicated in one's name is the next thing to immortality."

"I look forward to my afterlife in the literature of mucus."

"Oh, your image and reputation will survive intact. You're not looking at this properly. Don't you see what an opportunity this newt is? He's nearly providential. Snot on the hand, a pubic hair curled like script on linen, sperm shot across his lonely belly, his brains blown against a wall, it all speaks to Blanche. I say wind him up in the morning, watch him for a day and you'll never need another insight into the dirty human in your career."

197

"That's what I'm worried about. You think he's some sort of toy sent to corroborate your own most depraved ideas about the world."

Degas was curiously provoked by this. "Are you implying that I mean to harm my puppet? If so, you are mistaken. I couldn't hurt him even if I meant to. I believe two things about the world, and you overlook one of them. First, and this you are aware of, I believe that humans are beasts worse than beasts. Worse because they are idiotic beasts. A real beast is just itself and manages the whole affair of eating, shitting and dying with an admirable brevity and economy. But with a human there is always the pretense of angelic Reason. But this, as I say, you understand and you would agree with me if you weren't so preoccupied with the idea of being a great success, the supreme fop.

"However, you quite overlook my second belief. It is that God cares for Idiots and no matter how disastrously their lives turn out it is all still beautiful. For example, these ballerinas with their sour crotches and their hoary toes ripping through their tights and the procession of men young and otherwise lined up at their dressing rooms, their lives are calamities to the last one. Nonetheless, as my own paintings show, their failure is at the same time the transcendence of their failure."

"I don't understand."

"Of course you don't understand! You're an idiot! You never paint a stroke without thinking of the Masters. You have no idea what is happening right before your eyes. Compared to you, Louis Napoleon was a realist."

"And you think you describe people by saying that they smell!"

"Would you say they don't smell?"

"If one places the nose where you do, everything smells. What you need is a regular human relationship. What about Berthe

198

Morisot? She'd have you if you cared more about your dress and stopped plaguing her with your wit."

"I warn you, M. Manet, if you insult me I will become angry and there will be unpleasantness."

"I speak to you at all only because I care what becomes of the boy."

"Leave the boy to me."

"That's precisely what I don't want to do."

"Listen, go to a party with Proust, drink some champagne and mind your own business."

When little Blanche returned to his studio after his night out with Degas, it was nearly dawn. He felt humiliated and miserable. Why had Edgar been so cruel to him? What had he done to deserve it? He thought they were friends. But a friend doesn't call attention to the other's small weaknesses and peculiarities for the sake of general merriment, even if those around really are amused. An *education sublime* he kept calling it.

First there was all that damned Pernod. Ooh, really, his head hurt. And then that bawdy house. Degas had tried to buy a girl for him, but they had all refused. Except one who said that if he were cleaned a little she might consider it for an extra ten francs. And that Degas thought was the finest idea of all! A bath! Then before he could say a thing five or six of them were carrying him up the stairs, yanking at his pants and shoe strings.

Degas sat through the whole excruciating scene whistling and dashing off sketches. Finally, the bath was done and he was clean—except his genitals which no one would volunteer to scrub. He was given a towel to wrap himself in.

"Baths aren't free," said Degas, not even looking up from his sketch pad. "In this fine establishment, if you can not pay, you must sing; but since no one wishes to hear you sing, you must make one of your pretty speeches."

"Yes, a speech!" they howled.

"I'd prefer just to have my clothes back, please."

"And cheat these fine ladies!?"

"No, we refuse to be cheated," they agreed.

"So just a very little speech, Blanche. Say something about why you love these so-called Impressionists so much. What's wrong with our great French art of the past?"

"What! He doesn't like the great French art of the past?"

"Great French art!"

"Well, perhaps I can speak to that," said Blanche, shifting his weight in a cold puddle on the bathroom tiles. "The problem with the conservative art of the official salon is that it isn't any one person's art or vision, it is the State's art."

"We're a republic now. Are you criticizing the republic?" asked one.

"I believe he's one of those communards," said another.

"I have a friend in the ministry who would be interested in these ideas."

"Well, why should a painter have to imagine himself in eighteenth century Florence, in the Athens of Pericles, or the battlefields of Napoleon in order to have a canvas accepted?" Blanche warmed to his topic as he always did, in spite of the situation. "These paintings are made at all only because the bourgeoisie has...."

"Ooh, la la. The bourgeoisie, is it?"

"...Yes, the damnable bourgeoisie pays for it. So, the sole value the pictures really represent is money."

"He only speaks badly of money because he hasn't any."

"It is the Imagination of Commerce," Blanche insisted. ("The Imagination of Commerce" was his favorite phrase, and when he used it he felt at the very pinnacle of theoretical insight.)

"Here, five francs if you'll drop your towel."

"*Cul, mouches, merde, peau sale,*" whispered Degas. "Asshole. Flies. Shit. Dirty skin."

"May I please go?"

"No! No!" the ladies all complained. "It's our turn now. There are games to play. King of the Meat!"

"Yes! King of the Meat!"

"And the Old Rugged Crotch!"

"We haven't had anyone to play the Old Rugged Crotch with in ever so long!"

"But first, Blanche, please, more of your fancy idiocy," pleaded Degas, "I beg of you. I love it so."

When he thought about it, Blanche knew that they were wrong to have treated him so badly. But it made him think, what kind of person did you have to be before people could treat you with such contempt? He'd never heard of this happening to anyone else. So, even if it was wrong of them to treat him as they had, they could still be right. Oh, the gods, he knew they were right. He was stupid! A perfect dope!

This wasn't the sort of insight he desired. He threw himself on to the floor, noticing as he arrived there that he hadn't swept in some time. He picked a bit of feather, hair and loose dust from his mouth. This was the worst. He became conscious of his organs piled in his body like cheap goods in a grocery sack. But then he lifted his head. Wait a minute! He may have been stupid, of course he was stupid, an utter baba, he understood that now perfectly. But was there no value in the perfection of that understanding? He felt he had so much insight now into his essential brainlessness that he was really quite smart about that. Ho-ho! He put his hand on his crotch and gave himself a little squeeze of congratulation as he often did when he was pleased with himself. Wait till the fellows at the Guerbois heard this one!

Yes, this was really quite a nice moment. It would keep him going for awhile.

Quickly, then, he jumped to his feet and paced around his studio. He sat before his present canvas. It was a painting of a field of grass, with a road going through it and a haystack. The problem with this *pleine aire* style was that there was the devil of a lot of painting to do. Monet had been talking to him about painting ordinary things like haystacks, only he said he didn't know how to do it yet. He hoped Monet would be pleased when he showed him that it was possible even now to paint a haystack. It really did look like a haystack. It was a damned good haystack. One any cow would be happy to eat. He'd even put in some single blades of hay with a tiny brush and some kind of brown paint.

God he was pleased. He strode to the window, threw back the shutter and it was morning. He half expected to see a haystack out the window, but it was only Madame Rotisserie's boulangerie crouching as it always did on the opposite side of the road. But in this ecstatic first light even it looked beautiful. Then, he noticed the most marvelous thing: the air was full of hay which was falling like snow, gently quilting Paris. He laughed as he had when he was a child and his little village was visited by hay storms. He put his hand out and caught one. It really smelled like a barn. They say every piece of straw is unique, no two the same. This was a perfect day. He forgave Degas with all his heart.

Now it was getting chilly and he felt sleepy. But just before he closed the shutter, on a silly impulse he stuck out his childish tongue and caught a little of the chaff on it. It was just as sweet as he remembered.

SELECTED DALKEY ARCHIVE PAPERBACKS

PIERRE ALBERT-BIROT, *Grabinoulor.*
YUZ ALESHKOVSKY, *Kangaroo.*
FELIPE ALFAU, *Chromos.*
   Locos.
   Sentimental Songs.
IVAN ÂNGELO, *The Celebration.*
   The Tower of Glass.
ALAN ANSEN, *Contact Highs: Selected Poems 1957-1987.*
DAVID ANTIN, *Talking.*
DJUNA BARNES, *Ladies Almanack.*
   Ryder.
JOHN BARTH, *LETTERS.*
   Sabbatical.
SVETISLAV BASARA, *Chinese Letter.*
ANDREI BITOV, *Pushkin House.*
LOUIS PAUL BOON, *Chapel Road.*
ROGER BOYLAN, *Killoyle.*
IGNÁCIO DE LOYOLA BRANDÃO, *Zero.*
CHRISTINE BROOKE-ROSE, *Amalgamemnon.*
BRIGID BROPHY, *In Transit.*
MEREDITH BROSNAN, *Mr. Dynamite.*
GERALD L. BRUNS,
   Modern Poetry and the Idea of Language.
GABRIELLE BURTON, *Heartbreak Hotel.*
MICHEL BUTOR, *Degrees.*
   Mobile.
   Portrait of the Artist as a Young Ape.
G. CABRERA INFANTE, *Three Trapped Tigers.*
JULIETA CAMPOS, *The Fear of Losing Eurydice.*
ANNE CARSON, *Eros the Bittersweet.*
CAMILO JOSÉ CELA, *The Family of Pascual Duarte.*
   The Hive.
LOUIS-FERDINAND CÉLINE, *Castle to Castle.*
   London Bridge.
   North.
   Rigadoon.
HUGO CHARTERIS, *The Tide Is Right.*
JEROME CHARYN, *The Tar Baby.*
MARC CHOLODENKO, *Mordechai Schamz.*
EMILY HOLMES COLEMAN, *The Shutter of Snow.*
ROBERT COOVER, *A Night at the Movies.*
STANLEY CRAWFORD, *Some Instructions to My Wife.*
ROBERT CREELEY, *Collected Prose.*
RENÉ CREVEL, *Putting My Foot in It.*
RALPH CUSACK, *Cadenza.*
SUSAN DAITCH, *L.C.*
   Storytown.
NIGEL DENNIS, *Cards of Identity.*
PETER DIMOCK,
   A Short Rhetoric for Leaving the Family.
ARIEL DORFMAN, *Konfidenz.*
COLEMAN DOWELL, *The Houses of Children.*
   Island People.
   Too Much Flesh and Jabez.
RIKKI DUCORNET, *The Complete Butcher's Tales.*
   The Fountains of Neptune.
   The Jade Cabinet.
   Phosphor in Dreamland.
   The Stain.
WILLIAM EASTLAKE, *The Bamboo Bed.*
   Castle Keep.
   Lyric of the Circle Heart.
JEAN ECHENOZ, *Chopin's Move.*
STANLEY ELKIN, *A Bad Man.*
   Boswell: A Modern Comedy.
   Criers and Kibitzers, Kibitzers and Criers.
   The Dick Gibson Show.
   The Franchiser.
   George Mills.

   The Living End.
   The MacGuffin.
   The Magic Kingdom.
   Mrs. Ted Bliss.
   The Rabbi of Lud.
   Van Gogh's Room at Arles.
ANNIE ERNAUX, *Cleaned Out.*
LAUREN FAIRBANKS, *Muzzle Thyself.*
   Sister Carrie.
LESLIE A. FIEDLER,
   Love and Death in the American Novel.
FORD MADOX FORD, *The March of Literature.*
CARLOS FUENTES, *Terra Nostra.*
   Where the Air Is Clear.
JANICE GALLOWAY, *Foreign Parts.*
   The Trick Is to Keep Breathing.
WILLIAM H. GASS, *The Tunnel.*
   Willie Masters' Lonesome Wife.
ETIENNE GILSON, *The Arts of the Beautiful.*
   Forms and Substances in the Arts.
C. S. GISCOMBE, *Giscome Road.*
   Here.
DOUGLAS GLOVER, *Bad News of the Heart.*
KAREN ELIZABETH GORDON, *The Red Shoes.*
GEORGI GOSPODINOV, *Natural Novel.*
PATRICK GRAINVILLE, *The Cave of Heaven.*
HENRY GREEN, *Blindness.*
   Concluding.
   Doting.
   Nothing.
JIŘÍ GRUŠA, *The Questionnaire.*
JOHN HAWKES, *Whistlejacket.*
AIDAN HIGGINS, *A Bestiary.*
   Flotsam and Jetsam.
   Langrishe, Go Down.
ALDOUS HUXLEY, *Antic Hay.*
   Crome Yellow.
   Point Counter Point.
   Those Barren Leaves.
   Time Must Have a Stop.
MIKHAIL IOSSEL AND JEFF PARKER, EDS., *Amerika:*
   Contemporary Russians View the United States.
GERT JONKE, *Geometric Regional Novel.*
JACQUES JOUET, *Mountain R.*
HUGH KENNER, *Flaubert, Joyce and Beckett:*
   The Stoic Comedians.
DANILO KIŠ, *Garden, Ashes.*
   A Tomb for Boris Davidovich.
TADEUSZ KONWICKI, *A Minor Apocalypse.*
   The Polish Complex.
ELAINE KRAF, *The Princess of 72nd Street.*
JIM KRUSOE, *Iceland.*
EWA KURYLUK, *Century 21.*
VIOLETTE LEDUC, *La Bâtarde.*
DEBORAH LEVY, *Billy and Girl.*
   Pillow Talk in Europe and Other Places.
JOSÉ LEZAMA LIMA, *Paradiso.*
OSMAN LINS, *Avalovara.*
   The Queen of the Prisons of Greece.
ALF MAC LOCHLAINN, *The Corpus in the Library.*
   Out of Focus.
RON LOEWINSOHN, *Magnetic Field(s).*
D. KEITH MANO, *Take Five.*
BEN MARCUS, *The Age of Wire and String.*
WALLACE MARKFIELD, *Teitlebaum's Window.*
   To an Early Grave.
DAVID MARKSON, *Reader's Block.*
   Springer's Progress.
   Wittgenstein's Mistress.

FOR A FULL LIST OF PUBLICATIONS, VISIT:
www.dalkeyarchive.com

SELECTED DALKEY ARCHIVE PAPERBACKS

FOR A FULL LIST OF PUBLICATIONS, VISIT:
www.dalkeyarchive.com